"How far will you go to keep your fiancé happy?"

Stephanie's body stiffened with outrage, her mind exploding with anger. "I wouldn't try to charm you if you were the last man on earth." She added furiously, "I don't even like you. I hate you!"

There was a moment of strained silence, then Luke dragged her against him and began kissing her with a demanding hunger. She felt a deep response trigger inside her, as an urgent primeval passion flared between them. After endless moments, Luke raised his head and stared down at her flushed face.

She felt raw, defenseless and very guilty. She had been asked by her fiancé to use her charms on Luke. Her thoughts were in turmoil, but one thing was certain: Luke Baroda had the power to destroy her.

Books By Patricia Lake

PATRICIA LAKE

illusion of love

Harlequin Books

TORONTO • NEW YORK • LONDON
AMSTERDAM • PARIS • SYDNEY • HAMBURG
STOCKHOLM • ATHENS • TOKYO • MILAN

Harlequin Presents first edition July 1984
ISBN 0-373-10707-2

Original hardcover edition published in 1984
by Mills & Boon Limited

CHAPTER ONE

STEPHANIE walked along the pale beach lost in thought. The letter that had arrived in the morning post lay folded carefully in the pocket of her jeans.

Around her stretched the arc of sand, still cool beneath her bare feet, though it would be unbearably hot in a few hours' time. And at the edge of the beach the tall palm trees hissed quietly in the faint early morning breeze, shading the haphazard row of brightly-painted beach houses that always looked as though they were creeping towards the ocean.

She walked slowly, her face serious, frowning, deep in thought, hardly conscious of the beauty of her surroundings.

She walked along the beach every morning. It was the best time, cool and empty, the salty smell of the water and the clean air clearing her mind. Running into infinity at her side, the ocean usually had the power to calm her, the water a cool clear green as it licked up the sand, stretching darker to the azure horizon. Not today, it seemed.

It was three months since her father's funeral. She could not think of him without painful sadness, and now this letter from her half-sister Carina posed problems and demanded decisions that she was in no mood to tackle.

A jogger, tall and tanned, shot past her, shouting a friendly greeting. She watched his retreating back, wondering if she knew him. He looked vaguely familiar.

She sighed and stared up to the cloudless sky. This

tiny island was a tropical paradise and it promised another hot day. Contrarily, Stephanie longed for coolness—sometimes you could have too much of a good thing. I must pull myself together, she thought, and pushed the blonde silk of her hair back over her shoulders. Who could moan, living in a place such as this?

She walked briskly back towards the beach house, her expression determined, and ten minutes later was sitting by the open windows, drinking coffee and re-reading Carina's letter.

'You're up early.' Connie's husky voice brought Stephanie out of her reverie and she turned to smile at the girl who shared the rented beach house with her.

'I have to go to England,' she said, without preamble. 'I've had a letter from Carina.'

'You're going today?' Connie poured herself some coffee and yawned.

'No,' Stephanie laughed. 'Not today.'

'No problem, then,' Connie said practically, and sat down, closing her eyes.

Stephanie sighed again. Connie was right; there was no problem at all, no reason for her bleak mood.

'Okay, what's the matter?' Connie was watching her now, the coffee having brought her back to life.

'Oh, I don't know.' Stephanie got restlessly to her feet, moving across the room, unable to pin down her feelings. 'I feel miserable and unsettled. This letter . . .' She shrugged, breaking off. 'I don't know.'

'Why do you have to go to England, anyway?'

'Some legal business, my father's estate, the will . . .' Stephanie said vaguely. 'The letter is over there—read it.'

Connie reached for it, her eyes skimming the brief delicate writing. 'Why don't you want to go?' she asked curiously. 'Don't you get on with her?'

'I haven't seen her for ten years, I was only eleven when we left England. I don't suppose we will get on though,' Stephanie said pessimistically. 'We always were miles apart.'

Carina had been eighteen when Stephanie's mother and father had divorced. Stephanie and her mother had left England for this small, French-controlled Pacific island of Moahu, where her mother had distant relatives, almost immediately after the much-publicised, bitterly-contested divorce came through. Carina, the child of a previous marriage, had stayed behind with her father. Even at eighteen, she had been cold and very beautiful, the age difference and a certain amount of jealousy between the two girls always keeping them distant.

It had been a strange, distressing time that Stephanie could still remember vividly, and during the past ten years she had heard nothing from Carina or her father.

Against her mother's wishes, she had written regularly to her father, but had received no reply to any of her letters, only impersonal cards and presents at Christmas and birthdays.

Her mother had died when Stephanie was sixteen. She had known that her mother's solicitors had informed her father, and she had hoped that he would want to see her. No invitation was forthcoming, however, her only reply being a solicitor's letter informing her of a legal settlement made by her father.

And that had convinced her once and for all that he did not care. He had expelled Stephanie and her mother from his life completely, as though they did not exist. He did not want his sixteen-year-old daughter, only his sense of responsibility forced him to ensure that she was financially comfortable. For Stephanie it had been a savage blow, one that had left her deeply hurt and, although she had fought against it, faintly bitter.

Luckily she had been taken in by her mother's relatives; Dean had insisted on that.

They were second cousins. He was eight years older than her and they had grown up together. Now they were engaged and he was waiting for her to name the wedding day. He was the one man who cared for her, who had looked after her since she was a child. The years had bound them together. Dean had always comforted her and Stephanie had always loved him.

She smiled now as she thought of him, gazing down at the huge, brilliant sapphire ring on her wedding finger. 'It matches your beautiful eyes,' he had told her with a smile.

'Ten years is a long time, I guess,' Connie said thoughtfully, staring at her friend.

'I'll have to go, though,' Stephanie said with another sigh. 'Let's hope it won't take too long to sort out.' She looked at the clock on the table. 'You're going to be late, you know.'

Connie jumped to her feet, her wild red hair glinting in the sunlight. 'Oh God, I can't afford to be late again!' she wailed, and disappeared into the bedroom in panic.

Connie worked in one of the new hotel blocks on Moahu, which was fast becoming a chic international resort. She and Stephanie had been friends since their schooldays at the island convent school. Connie was American, her family brought to the island by her father's engineering work. She was tall and slim with a red-haired beauty and a hard edge to her personality that gave her a calm, philosophical view of the world.

Stephanie, on the other hand, was vulnerable, very sensitive and frankly envious of Connie's carefree attitude to life.

Connie left ten minutes later, whirling from the beach house, the door slamming behind her. Smiling, Stephanie poured herself more coffee and stared out over the hazy ocean, glad that she did not have to work today.

She worked part-time, as a secretary to a novelist, Bertha Channing, who was at present travelling through India and not expected back for some months. The job suited her perfectly, as her employer's frequent travelling gave Stephanie the time to paint, her first love.

She painted landscapes for money. They sold well to the richer tourists. And for herself, she painted portraits, of friends, pictures of her favourite places on the island. She knew without conceit that she was good—very talented, but today, she was in no mood for painting, for anything.

She still felt apprehensive about visiting England, although she did not know why. Her father's rejection still hurt her, and she was still afraid to examine that pain too closely. Perhaps that was the cause of her unrest.

And there was Carina—how would she greet Stephanie after all these years? The letter was hardly affectionate, hardly welcoming. Stephanie understood now that Carina had been jealous of her, of her mother. The older girl had been afraid that her special position in her father's affections would be usurped by his new wife and their daughter. Looking back with the insight she now possessed, Stephanie could see that her father, not deliberately, of course, had been uncaring of Carina's fears.

It was obvious that Carina had felt an outsider, which explained her coldness, her jealousy. But understanding the situation did not make it any easier to cope with, and Stephanie had no idea how her half-sister would receive her.

She cleared away the coffee cups, tidied the beach house, then sunbathed without enthusiasm, her mind ticking over the whole time, until it was time to meet Dean for lunch. He owned a casino in the town, and she drove along the coast road in her white sports car, the breeze tangling her fine blonde hair, for once not noticing the beauty of her surroundings.

She stopped at a red light, her eyes fixed blindly on the lush palm trees, the profusion of hibiscus flowers, still thinking. Perhaps Dean would go with her to England. She would ask him over lunch.

As the plan formed in her mind, she was suddenly aware of somebody watching her. The awareness was so strong that the hair prickled on the back of her neck. She absently turned her head. There was a long black car beside hers, waiting for the lights to change. Her eyes met those of the man in the car and their glances locked with a strange ferocity.

His eyes were green, warm, with a lazy, sensual charm that caught Stephanie's breath. She stared at him, blind to everything else. She couldn't look away. Her heart seemed to have stopped beating, she realised in panic, relieved when she felt it starting to pound heavily. She felt as though she was drowning in the warm depths of those green eyes, her mind suddenly blank, her own eyes wide and innocent. There was a shock reverberating through her body as she understood the invitation, the powerful magnetism of this stranger's charm. Nothing like this had ever happened to her before. She had never looked at a man and experienced such awareness of herself, of him.

A loud, impatient car horn behind her brought her to her senses. The lights were green. Stephanie broke the eye contact, hot colour flushing her cheeks as she released the handbrake and shot the car forward.

What on earth was the matter with her? She was

used to men staring at her, used to blatant invitations from insistent strangers. She knew without conceit that she was beautiful, her hair long, pale and shining, her face perfect and delicately-boned, her curved body tanned and attractive.

This man had been different, though. She had known that despite her lack of experience. There had been a sureness in his eyes, a self-assurance, a promise.

She tried to remember his face, but she had looked only into his eyes, a vague impression of lean dark features and a hard mouth, all that remained in her memory.

An unimportant incident that had lasted only a few seconds—that's all it was, she told herself sternly. But the images remained as she drove along the sun-drenched coast, images of those warm green eyes that had held hers so effortlessly. And she couldn't help wondering who he was, even though she longed to shake the incident from her mind. It was too disturbing to be so affected by a total stranger. She was engaged to Dean; she should not even be looking at any other man.

Impatient with her own foolishness, she screeched the car to a halt outside the casino and walked quickly inside.

Dean was in the offices, talking to Camil and another one of his men, smiling as he saw her. Stephanie smiled back, watching him as he dismissed the men and came towards her. He was tall and lithe and good-looking, his hair bleached by the sun, his smile lazy, carefree. She felt reassured by his familiarity, flinging her arms around his neck and kissing him.

He responded urgently, pulling her against his body, his blue eyes heating as he looked down at her.

'Pleased to see me, honey?' he asked teasingly.

'Of course, I am,' she smiled, while those green eyes forced their image into her mind again, tormenting her, irritating her. 'And I'm ravenous!' She wondered at her own restless lie. 'Are you ready to take me to lunch?'

'Sure, come on.' He slid his arm around her waist and they strolled out of the casino, across the narrow road to a favourite restaurant. They ordered fish, a local speciality, and rice. Stephanie found she could hardly touch the beautifully prepared food.

Dean ordered wine and she drank more than usual, her small face becoming flushed as the meal wore on. Her own mood perplexed her. She watched Dean as though she had never seen him before. He meant everything to her. He was her brother, her father, her fiancé. He had shaped her adolescent personality with his carefree charm, the drive that made him so successful. Yet as she watched him over the meal, she realised for the first time that she had always held part of herself back.

They had not become lovers. Dean wanted her, he did not bother to disguise his desire for her, but he had never pushed her, and she would have had to have been pushed. She loved him, but there was no need burning inside her. She could wait until they were married.

A frown pleated her smooth forehead. Was that how love was supposed to be? Shouldn't it be fierce and urgent? Again, those smiling green eyes insinuated themselves into her memory and she shook her head as though physically trying to dislodge the disturbing images. She loved Dean. She *loved* him.

He was talking about the casino, she realised. She had not been listening, and she gave herself away.

He smiled at her, indulgence in his eyes. 'You haven't been listening to a word I've said, have you?'

Stephanie sipped her wine. 'Do you have a cigarette?' she countered sweetly.

'Sure.' He lit one for her and placed it between her lips, the gesture intimate. 'What's the matter, honey? You've been in a daze all through lunch.'

'I've had a letter from my half-sister. I have to go over to England to sort out some details of my father's estate with his solicitors,' she explained briefly.

For just a second, she saw something in Dean's face, something strange, alien, then his eyes narrowed speculatively. 'You mean I may be engaged to an heiress?' There was laughter in his voice. He did not understand.

'I don't want to go,' she told him earnestly.

'Why not? Think of it as a holiday. Buy yourself some clothes in London—you'll need something for the wedding.' His eyes smiled, but beneath the smile she saw that urgency again, brought on by the thought of their wedding, an urgency she could not match within herself however hard she tried.

'Will you come with me?' she asked quickly, seriously, hoping that he would see how important it was. He was flattered, his ego boosted by her need. She could see that as he reached across the table and took her hand in his.

'I'm not sure I can spare the time right now, honey—you know how it is. When are you going?'

'This week. I want to go as soon as possible, I don't want it hanging over me . . .'

Dean already knew about her father and Carina. He must know how she felt, what it meant to her. Her dark blue eyes pleaded with him, but he wasn't even looking at her. He was thinking hard.

'There's no way I can spare the time at the moment, Stephanie,' he finally said, regretfully. 'The word's out that Luke Baroda flew in yesterday. If he's thinking of buying in, I want to be here.'

Stephanie wasn't listening. 'Dean——'

'Look, are you expecting any trouble from Carina? Do you think she might contest the will?'

'No, no, nothing like that.' Her voice was miserable. It seemed that his mind was made up; he couldn't spare the time. 'I just hoped you would come with me.'

Dean lifted his shoulders. 'I'm sorry honey, it's a bad time, that's all. You go—enjoy yourself.'

She nodded in silence. She supposed she was being unreasonable expecting him to drop everything at a moment's notice. He was, after all, a busy man and there was nothing in England that she could not handle herself.

'No, I'm sorry.' She smiled suddenly. 'I know how rushed you are.'

Dean relaxed, smiling back, his eyes intent on her beautiful face. 'You'll be back before you know it,' he said lightly, sounding dismissive to her over-sensitive ears.

He kissed her passionately as they left the restaurant. 'Have dinner with me tonight. We can eat at the Casino,' he murmured against her cheek.

Guilty at her own thoughts over lunch, Stephanie agreed immediately, 'Yes, I'd like that.'

'I'll pick you up at eight.' He kissed her again and was gone.

Stephanie stood by her car for a moment, wondering how to spend the rest of the afternoon. She knew the mood she was in meant that she would be unable to settle to anything, so she wandered around the shops, stopping mid-afternoon for a long, cool drink at a café on the beach, chatting to the owner's wife whom she knew well.

It was a lazy, disorganised afternoon, and she walked for miles before driving home.

Connie was at the beach house when she returned, her feet up, her eyes closed.

'Finished for the day?' Stephanie asked sympathetically.

'You've got to be kidding—I'm back on duty in two and a half hours. We're not all ladies of leisure, you know.'

'I'm only one until Bertha gets back, and besides, you know you love it.'

'At this moment, believe me, I don't! My feet are *killing* me. If it gets any busier, I'm going to hand in my notice!'

Stephanie laughed and went off to take a bath.

She dressed carefully for dinner with Dean, choosing a daring black dress that clung to the perfect curves of her body. She brushed out her long hair and left it loose to drift silkily around her bare shoulders, then lightly made up her face.

Dean whistled long and low when he saw her, staring, reaching for her, his fingers eagerly tracing the soft lines of her shoulders.

'You look fantastic,' he said hoarsely as he raised his mouth from hers.

'Thank you.' Stephanie smiled at him, hating herself for being almost unmoved by his kiss. What was happening to her? She moved away to collect her handbag. 'I'm ready.'

She watched the ocean as they drove to the casino, chatting absently to Dean. She would book her flight to London tomorrow morning. Perhaps once she had been to England, she would feel like her normal self again. She hated feeling the way she did at the moment; it ruined everything.

The restaurant was full, she noticed, as Dean led her to his table. It had an excellent reputation, and business was booming. A band played in one corner, behind the dance floor, well-dressed couples dancing to the slow, discreet music.

Stephanie ordered a gin and tonic and looked around with interest. The atmosphere in the restaurant was totally different from that in the gaming rooms. Here there was laughter, a relaxed air, talking and dancing. In the gaming rooms there was an intensity, a stillness, a greed in the carefully blank faces of the players.

Stephanie never gambled, the idea held no appeal for her—she hardly ever went into the other rooms. One of Dean's men appeared by his side as they were ordering, whispering in his ear. Dean rose immediately. 'I'm sorry, honey—I'll be back in a moment.'

She smiled, nodding, used to him being called away when they ate here. She sipped her drink and ordered her meal, even though she didn't feel very hungry.

She idly watched the other diners, easily picking out the serious gamblers—a game she often played. Mostly men, there was an impatience about them, a boredom with their surroundings. They frightened her a little, they were so singlemindedly obsessed, and she pitied the beautiful women who sat so languidly with them.

As promised, Dean returned within minutes.

'Sorted the problem out?' Stephanie asked with a smile, suddenly feeling a rush of affection for him. He was so dear to her, she was closer to him than to anybody else in the world.

She saw the gleaming brightness in his eyes, his love of his work. 'You wouldn't believe it,' he said with a kind of restless excitement in his voice, 'but Luke Baroda is playing the tables. He hasn't lost a franc. That guy has the devil's own luck—he's winning thousands!'

'Luke Baroda?' Stephanie echoed vaguely. The name sounded familiar. Hadn't Dean mentioned him over lunch? She hadn't been listening.

'Luke Baroda,' Dean repeated patiently. 'The property tycoon. He owns chains of hotels in practically every country in the world. I've asked him to join us for a drink later—you don't mind, do you, honey?'

'No, of course not,' She accepted it gracefully as part of Dean's work, although she usually disliked these rich gamblers he introduced her to.

The food arrived at that moment and Dean ate heartily, not noticing that Stephanie barely touched a thing on her plate.

The waiters hovered round them and she sipped her wine, hoping that Dean was not going to play with this property tycoon. There was a wild, reckless streak in Dean, usually well under control, that frightened her. He saw the rare, successful gamblers as a sort of personal challenge. He wanted to beat them, he needed to beat them, and he had lost hundreds of thousands of francs trying.

Stephanie had only watched one of these big games and she had walked out halfway through, unable to bear the tension, the silence, or the shock that the Dean who sat at the table risking huge sums of money was a stranger to her. She had seen a side of his personality that was totally unknown to her that night. He had been completely unaware of her presence, his eyes fixed, his face filmed with sweat. She shivered now, as she thought about it.

The meal finished, they drank coffee and brandy, their conversation light and lazy. Then Stephanie stood up. 'Excuse me,' She smiled at Dean and made for the ladies' room, where she brushed out her hair and checked her make-up.

She stared at herself in the long gilt-edged mirrors. She looked cool, composed, her fair hair tumbling around her shoulders. That strange mood still sat on her, changing her viewpoint on life, somehow changing everything.

Another woman entered the room as she was examining her reflection, middle-aged, beautifully-coiffured, her wrists and throat glittering with diamonds.

Stephanie smiled and left, to make her way back to the table. There was a man sitting with Dean now, his back to her as she approached. He had wide, powerful shoulders, she noted, not concealed by the expensively-tailored white dinner jacket he wore.

His hair was almost black, thick, touching the white collar in stark contrast. Dean was talking, his face earnest, respectful.

So this was the big winner, the property tycoon— Luke somebody-or-other. At least he had good shoulders, Stephanie thought wryly—which was more than could be said for most of them. Dean was falling over himself to impress, and she sighed as she reached his side.

Both men rose. Dean slid his arm around her shoulders, his fingers caressing her bare skin, blatantly possessive.

'Stephanie, I'd like you to meet Luke Baroda.' To the man, he smiled, 'Stephanie Maxwell, my fiancée.'

Stephanie pinned a polite smile on her face and held out her hand. But the breath caught in her throat as she looked up into lazy, hooded green eyes. He was the disturbing stranger at the traffic lights!

Her smile disappeared. She felt panicky. His hand, strong and tanned, closed around hers.

'Miss Maxwell,' He inclined his head, the light gleaming in his nearly-black hair, his mouth faintly amused. She knew he remembered the incident that afternoon.

'How ... How do you do, Mr Baroda.' Her voice came out small and stupidly breathless. He was tall, taller than Dean, his body lean and powerful. She had to tilt back her head to look into his face.

He released her hand and they sat down. He and Dean were talking, but Stephanie wasn't listening. She glanced covertly at him. His face was hard, serious, the soft lighting in the restaurant emphasising the lean angles of his bones, the strength of his jaw, the shadows beneath his cheekbones. His mouth was firm and sensual, promising expertise. He was very, very attractive, there was something about him that riveted her attention.

He turned his head suddenly and caught her looking at him. He did not smile, simply stared at her, and Stephanie, unable to drag her eyes away, felt the colour pouring into her cheeks. Those eyes were incredible, she thought shakily, mesmerising, faintly cynical, charming. She looked into them and saw his strength, his self-assurance, a potent sexuality that made her colour rise higher and her stomach turn over.

She leaned closer to Dean as though seeking protection from this dark, somehow threatening stranger.

'Would you care to dance, Miss Maxwell?' Luke Baroda's voice was low, almost expressionless, and she heard the question with something akin to fear trembling inside her.

She looked at Dean. 'I. ... No, I. ...' She needed an excuse to refuse. Dean, say something! she thought desperately.

Luke Baroda watched her, reading her mind. 'I'm sure your fiancé won't object to one dance,' he drawled mockingly, in challenge.

Dean laughed, patting her arm. 'Go ahead, honey,' he said lightly, carefully. Very clever, Stephanie thought bitterly as she stood up and allowed Luke Baroda to steer her on to the dance floor.

She did not look up at him, but felt the light touch of his hand against her waist as they began to move to the music. Luke Baroda held her closely, the dance floor was crowded, enforcing their intimacy. She felt the muscles of his shoulder tensing beneath her hand, inhaled the clean male scent of his body mingling with a faint attractive cologne.

She could hear her heart beating faster than usual, her throat aching with a strange tension. She wanted to get away—away from him. He was dangerous. She didn't know how she knew that, but she did. He was staring down at her, unnerving her. She did not look up.

'You dance superbly,' he said, his voice amused, his mouth close to her hair.

'Thank you.' It was he who was dancing superbly, she was merely following.

She dared to look up at him then, and her heart began to pound.

'Are . . . are you here on holiday?' she asked, for something to say, not really interested.

'Why do you ask? You don't give a damn,' he replied coolly.

'Polite conversation, Mr Baroda—something you obviously know little about.'

Her suddenly-angry eyes met his, and incredibly, he smiled, his mouth curving, etching deep lines in his tanned face.

'You're very beautiful,' he said softly, his green eyes lazily assessing. Stephanie felt herself blushing, jumping as his hard thigh accidently brushed hers.

'Flattery?' she queried scornfully.

'Polite conversation, Miss Maxwell. Isn't that what you wanted?' He was teasing her, and despite herself, she felt a smile tugging at her lips.

Luke Baroda's eyes narrowed on that smile and as their eyes met again, they were both suddenly serious, a powerful tension crackling between them, cutting them off from the rest of the room, from the rest of the world.

The music had stopped, she realised moments later. Luke Baroda's hands dropped from her body and they made their way back to the table.

Dean was smiling as they sat down. He looked pleased, Stephanie thought, and slid her hand into his, relieved that the dance was over. There was something about Luke Baroda that worried her, though it was purely instinctive. He knew too much. She had never met anyone quite like him before.

He was watching her now, as she leaned towards Dean, his eyes narrowed, assessing.

She wanted to go. But Dean was still going all out to impress and Stephanie could see that Luke Baroda was totally aware of Dean's tactics. Her dislike of him grew as she saw the cynicism in his eyes. She felt totally panic-stricken when Dean rose to take an important telephone call in his office. She felt the ridiculous urge to run after him. There was no way she wanted to be left alone with this tall, powerful stranger, and glancing at him, she was aware that he knew how she was feeling.

He stared at her, noting the nervous way her hands played with her glass, the flickering of her eyelids. He glanced at the sapphire engagement ring on her finger and asked casually, 'How long have you been engaged?'

He was making polite conversation again, she thought, but at least this was safe ground.

'Six months,' she replied, flashing him a brief, polite smile before looking away.

His face was expressionless. 'And when will you be getting married?'

'We haven't set the date yet.' Her voice was cold. She felt very defensive. Luke Baroda smiled, as though he found her answer amusing, but said nothing.

Stephanie watched as he lit a cigar, watched the fragrant smoke drifting from his lips. There was an unhurried grace in all his actions that inexplicably alarmed her. He was too sure.

'How long have you known Sangster?'

Stephanie frowned. Why was he asking all these questions? 'I've known Dean since I was a child—not that it's any of your business,' she added with a flash of daring.

'You're little more than a child now.' There was a sudden quality of tenderness in his voice that made her heart turn over.

'I'm twenty-one!' she told him indignantly, her breathing irregular and fast.

Luke Baroda smiled again, still staring at her intently. 'As old as that?' The green eyes mocked.

'I believe you won tonight,' she said politely, changing the subject, and stared away from him across the crowded room.

'I always win.'

'Always?' His calm arrogance infuriated her.

'Yes—hasn't your fiancé told you that?'

He was making fun of her and she glared at him. 'I——'

'I'm sorry, darling,' Dean was beside them. She had not even noticed his approach. 'This is going to take longer than I expected—I'll probably be tied up for the next hour or so.'

Consciously trying to ignore Luke Baroda's probing gaze, Stephanie stared up into Dean's face.

'I'll take a taxi home,' she said with a brilliant, fevered smile. There was no way she was going to spend the next hour in Luke Baroda's company. 'I'm a little tired, anyway. I'll see you tomorrow.'

Dean's eyes burned regretfully down into hers. 'Sure?'

'Yes, it's getting late.'

'I will be more than happy to give Miss Maxwell a life home.' Luke Baroda's cool voice cut between them like a knife, his suggestion shocking Stephanie to the core. She smiled slightly, a polite refusal hovering on her lips, but Dean would not allow it. He would refuse for her.

'Well, if you're sure. . . .' Her head jerked up in astonishment as she heard Dean's voice.

'My pleasure.' Luke Baroda sounded cool, uncaring.

Stephanie looked at Dean and saw his uncertainty. He didn't want her to go with Luke Baroda, but on the other hand, he could not refuse without appearing petty. Luke Baroda was an important, influential man, a man Dean needed to impress. Dean bent his fair head and slowly brushed Stephanie's lips with his own. It was a warning to the lean powerful man who watched the kiss with blank eyes.

'I'll ring you tomorrow, honey.'

Stephanie did not answer. She felt a stab of irritation at Dean's weakness and she certainly had no intention of letting Luke Baroda drive her home. She walked from the casino with her head held high, aware of the dark, disturbing man at her side. As the warm night air hit them, she turned to him, swallowing nervously as she looked into his dark shadowed face.

'There's really no need. . . .'

'Stephanie.' He placed a long, hard finger gently across her lips. 'It suits you.' He mused, a wicked amusement glinting in his eyes.

'Mr Baroda. . . .' She was shocked, trembling at his casual touch, yet held still by his magnetism, by the sheer force of his smile.

'You know my name, use it.'

'I . . . I want to get a taxi,' she muttered, very flustered.

'I'm driving you home,' he told her calmly, and sliding a hand beneath her elbow, guided her gently but firmly towards his low, black car.

'But I don't know you,' she said angrily, as she slid into a luxurious leather seat.

Luke Baroda slid in beside her seconds later and turned to her in the darkness.

'You have nothing to fear from me,' he said gently.

Stephanie stared at him, her heart beating very fast. She trusted him, she realised with a shock, trusted him and yet feared him—a crazy combination of feelings. So, defeatedly, she gave him her address, explaining how to get to the beach house, then settled back nervously into her seat as the powerful car roared into life, shooting out of town towards the coast road.

She was desperately aware of the man beside her as she stared blindly out through the windscreen, aware of every movement he made. She glanced at his hard profile from beneath her lashes. She could read no expression in his face at all. He was silent, seemingly preoccupied with his own thoughts.

She thought of Dean and sighed. He should have known that she did not want to be left alone with Luke Baroda. He should have known.

'*You* must have known that he wouldn't refuse.' Luke Baroda's cool ironic voice made her jump. She glared at him. Could he read her mind?

'I beg your pardon?' she said stiffly.

'You don't know him at all, do you?' His eyes met hers for a brief second, hard, intent, probing, and Stephanie's mouth tightened fiercely.

'Why don't you mind your own business?' she demanded.

'You don't deny it, then.' There was a cold amusement in the words.

'I don't have to deny anything. Dean and I are very close. . . .'

'But you're not lovers.'

'How the hell do you know?' She was so angry, her blue eyes glittered, her body turned in the seat towards him. Who did he think he was, anyway? A stranger who had no right to be making such personal remarks.

The car slowed, gliding to a standstill. She was home, she realised, and it had taken no time at all.

Luke Baroda looked at her angry little face and smiled.

'Oh, I know,' he said softly. 'You wear your innocence like a cloak.' He reached out his hand and touched her silken hair.

Stephanie felt her heart pounding, her mouth drying. She shook her head and his hand dropped. She felt utterly confused by what he had said to her.

'I don't understand. . . .' she whispered, caught in some strange spell that bound them together in the warm darkness of the car.

'No?' There was a moment's silence, then, 'You won't marry Sangster,' he told her in a cool, sure voice. 'Because I want you, Stephanie—and I always get what I want.'

Her eyes widened in pure alarm, a shuddering fire tearing through her body. The calm certainty in his voice and the darkness of his eyes spoke of premonition. Every word he had said was enforced by the hard lines of his face and she felt frightened to death.

'Go to hell!' she whispered shakily, and stumbling out of the car, ran towards the beach house as though the devil himself was after her.

CHAPTER TWO

LONDON was veiled in dull, grey rain when Stephanie arrived. She stared out of the tiny window on the plane and felt miserable. She had forgotten how grey London was. It was difficult to believe that above the heavy clouds through which the plane had ploughed on its descent, the sun shone in an incredibly blue and purple sunset sky.

Ten years was a long time, but she still remembered tiny details, like the smell of the English air, the dark light and the fact that it was so cold even though it was supposed to be summer time.

She pulled on her warm herringbone jacket and collected her belongings, leaving the plane with apprehension. She had telephoned Carina to inform her of the flight number and arrival time. Her half-sister had sounded distant, rather cool, which hadn't helped Stephanie's shaky confidence. Her encounter with Luke Baroda hadn't helped either.

She had dreamt of him every night since he had driven her home from the casino—harsh, vivid dreams that scared her. He was a powerful man, those dark forceful looks burned into her memory, impossible to forget. She had not seen him since that night. Dean had told her eagerly that he was on the other side of the island, negotiating a land deal, and Stephanie had breathed a sigh of relief on hearing that. By the time he got back she would be well on her way to England. She would not have to see him again.

She supposed in retrospect that she should have told Dean what Luke Baroda had said. She didn't. It would have sounded ridiculous in the telling, laughable without those cool eyes and that hard mouth to reinforce his meaning. And what could Dean have done? Stephanie had the uneasy, guilty feeling that Dean had no strength against Luke Baroda. And so she had said nothing, secretly still a little hurt at the calm way Dean had allowed Luke Baroda to drive her home.

Dean had given her a lift to the airport. He had been quiet, his mood obviously foul.

Sighing, Stephanie had patiently tried to find out the reason for his bad temper, and her tentative enquiries finally revealed that he had lost heavily at cards the night before. That had not helped her anxious mood. She knew Dean gambled almost compulsively, he did not hide it from her even though he knew she disapproved. He usually lost; he was too reckless to win any important game.

His mood had not lightened when he kissed her goodbye and promised to telephone. Ridiculous tears had welled up in her eyes as he left. She felt that it was unfair of him to take his mood out on her. It wasn't her fault, after all, if he lost in the casino.

She frowned as she collected her suitcase from the baggage carousel. Why was she so bad-tempered of late? Why was she letting tiny irrelevant things irritate her? She knew Dean inside out; she had always accepted the weakness she saw in him. It was part of his character, and she loved him as he was. The sooner her father's estate was sorted out, the better. Then she could get back to normal again. How many times had she said that to herself? Luke Baroda's dark face rose to mock her. If she was honest, wasn't he at the bottom of this tension inside her? Damn him!

She purposefully thrust him from her mind, looking around for her half-sister, but there was no sign of her. Surely Carina hadn't forgotten?

Stephanie set down her case and looked round helplessly. If Carina didn't turn up, she supposed she could hire a car and make her own way to the address on the letter. She hoped it wouldn't come to that. She pushed back her hair and frowned at a man who was staring fixedly at her from a few yards away. She felt very alone. About to make her way to the hired car office, she jumped as a hand touched her shoulder, and whirled round to find herself face to face with a tall, dark young man. She opened her mouth, about to freeze him off.

'Stephanie Maxwell?' he smiled, knowing from the look in her eyes that she had been about to bite his head off.

Stephanie looked at him warily. 'Yes, but . . .?'

'Carina got caught up with a phone call from her agent. I'm here to pick you up.' His voice was light and friendly, his face lean and attractive.

'Oh, I see. . . .' she smiled uncertainly at him.

'I'd better introduce myself—I'm Wayne.' He held out his hand and she took it. His was the first friendly face she'd seen since arriving in England and his smile was infectious.

'Hello, Wayne,' she laughed, feeling relieved.

He picked up her suitcase despite her protests and led her out into the cool, nearly-evening air. Stephanie shivered. It was cold and the rain didn't help, darkening the sky, hastening the night.

'Not used to the English summer, huh?' Wayne smiled, and helped her into a long red car.

'It's freezing!' she said emphatically.

'You're joking.' He slid in beside her and started the engine.

'How long since you've been here?'

'Ten years.' Stephanie stared out of the car windows, trying to remember her surroundings. None of the streets or the buildings triggered any memories.

'A long time.'

'Yes.' She was thinking of her father. She had not seen him for ten years either, and now it was much too late.

Wayne offered her a cigarette which she took, though she rarely smoked, and they chatted as the car left London on its way to the coast.

'You're not at all like Carina, are you?' Wayne commented, shooting her a glance from beneath his dark brows.

Stephanie shrugged. 'I don't know, I was only a child when my parents got divorced. . . .' Her voice trailed off. Had Wayne known her father? Was he Carina's boy-friend? She almost laughed. He could be Carina's husband for all she knew!

'Do you know Carina well?' she asked tentatively.

'Not particularly. She keeps me at arm's length unless I can be useful to her,' he replied without a trace of malice, almost as through the whole situation amused him. 'She knows what she wants, and I don't really fit into any of her plans, except perhaps as an errand boy.'

'Oh, I'm sorry. . . .'

'I didn't mean *that*,' he told her with mock exasperation. 'Now that I've met you, I'm glad I volunteered for the job. Besides, I wouldn't leave anybody standing waiting for Carina.'

The car suddenly slowed, pulling off the road. Wayne saw her enquiring eyes and said, 'I left the house in a hurry, and I don't know about you, but I could murder a cup of coffee.'

'Me too.' Stephanie slid out of the car, glad to stretch her legs.

It was almost dark, late in the evening now. The air smelled strange to her, heavy with car fumes instead of flowers and the sea. They walked into the roadside café and Wayne ordered two coffees, then they sat down near the window.

She looked at Wayne from beneath her lashes. She would have estimated that he was in his mid-twenties, perhaps a little older. His hair was dark, his eyes brown. He wore casual clothes, cord trousers and a leather jacket. She liked him, she decided, as their eyes met and he smiled.

'Nervous?'

Stephanie nodded, biting her lower lip.

'Carina's bark is much worse than her bite, remember that.' He took a mouthful of coffee and grimaced. 'Good God, I did order coffee, didn't I?'

Stephanie giggled. He was right—the coffee was weak and lukewarm and tasted of nothing in particular.

'It's just that I haven't seen her for so long. We're strangers really, and she didn't sound. . . .' She broke off abruptly. She did not know Wayne well enough to criticise Carina in front of him.

Wayne's eyes were sympathetic, though. 'Carina is as cold as ice and very self-contained—she's used to being alone, I think. Your father's death was quite a shock to her, although you wouldn't guess. She hides her feelings very cleverly and she doesn't seem particularly fond of women. I'm warning you now, so that you'll know it's nothing personal if the two of you don't hit it off.'

Stephanie smiled. Wayne obviously knew her half-sister very well, and she was curious to know what the relationship was between them. 'Thanks,' she said.

Wayne shrugged dramatically. 'Don't mention it.' He watched her as she pushed back her hair, his eye caught by the sapphire flashing on her finger. 'Hey, you're engaged!'

'Very observant!' she teased in reply.

'And I thought I might have a chance with you.' His eyes were unashamedly flirtatious, and Stephanie hoped that he wasn't too involved with Carina.

'Well, I'm spoken for.' She smiled at him, drawn by his warmth.

'I'm surprised the lucky man lets you out of his sight!'

Stephanie's face sobered as she thought of Dean and his coolness with her on the way to Moahu airport. 'He's very busy,' she explained, staring down into the murky depths of her coffee cup.

'What does he do?'

'He runs a casino,' she said coolly.

'I'm impressed.'

'What do you do?' she asked, wanting to change the subject.

Wayne smiled. 'I work for my cousin—nothing spectacular, I'm afraid, but it's an easy life and that's the way I like it.' His eyes glinted wickedly. 'I'm a lazy swine—I'm only telling you now because you're bound to find out if you're staying at the house.'

Stephanie couldn't help laughing. At least he was honest. And very charming—he would be an ally and probably a friend. 'I'm sure that's not true,' she said lightly.

'Ah, you wait and see.' He glanced at his watch. 'I suppose we ought to be moving—you must be tired and hungry.' He took her arm as they walked back to the car.

'Is it far now?' Stephanie stared out over the dark flat fields of the English countryside.

'About three-quarters of an hour's drive.'

She sat back in her seat, the warmth from the car heater relaxing her, making her drowsy. Wayne switched on the radio, and she listened to the quiet music, watched the flash of car headlights and the rapidly darkening sky.

Her childhood memories of England had been warped by time. There was nothing particularly welcoming or familiar in what she saw around her. It was not like coming home.

The house was near the sea, standing on tall jagged cliffs. An old house, Stephanie saw from the lights outside, a big house. It was made of stone, the windows three storeys high, the dark roof supporting tall chimneys. It was beautiful—she fell in love with it as soon as she saw it. It should have been bleak, standing so proud and alone on the high cliffs, but it wasn't, it was warm and special and welcoming.

She climbed stiffly from the warmth of the car, shivering as the night air hit her. It was damp, filled with the smell and the noise of the sea. Gulls screamed terrifyingly loud overhead. The front door was firmly shut—Carina obviously didn't intend to welcome her.

Wayne collected her suitcase from the boot. 'Come on.' His voice was encouraging; her loneliness and uncertainty were easy to read.

They walked up the front steps together, and here the scent was of wild roses, from the bushes surrounding the heavy wooden door. Inside, the house was warm and bright, as Stephanie had imagined it to be, and beautifully decorated, its stark simplicity taking her breath away. The hall was high, the walls pale melon, the wide staircase and the cantilevered floor polished wood. Her first impression was of huge paintings, of shining silver bowls of deeply coloured flowers, their scent filling the air, and of dark furniture. As they walked over richly patterned rugs, she felt herself smiling inside, responding to the beauty of the place, the atmosphere of calmness, of peace.

Wayne led her into a lounge where a huge fire roared and a slim, dark-haired woman rose with careful grace from a long, brilliantly-striped settee.

'So you've finally arrived! I imagine the journey was dreadful.'

Carina stretched out her pale, perfect hand, polite, unsmiling.

'Hello, Carina.' Stephanie's voice was husky as she took her half-sister's hand. Carina was breathtakingly beautiful, a total stranger.

'You look frozen—come nearer to the fire.' Her half-sister's voice was cool, but at least she was being kind, Stephanie thought ruefully. She moved closer to the carved fireplace, as instructed, warming her cold hands.

She looked down at her own tight jeans, then at Carina's exquisite silk jacquard suit in scarlet and blue, at the shining darkness of her half-sister's hair, the oval beauty of her face, and sighed silently. She and Carina were a million miles apart. There seemed no point of contact between them.

'I'm sure you could do with a drink.' Carina didn't smile, and her eyes slid assessingly over Stephanie's slender body in a slightly disapproving way.

'Some coffee would be lovely. I am a little cold,' Stephanie replied tentatively.

'The weather broke yesterday—the summer has been very hot,' Carina said coolly, and turned to Wayne, who had watched the two girls greeting each other, with wise, amused eyes. 'Wayne, be a darling and ask Rose to make some coffee.'

'Sure,' He smiled crookedly at Stephanie and left the room.

'Cigarette?' Carina held out an elegantly-engraved case. Stephanie shook her head and Carina said amusedly, 'Don't hover, darling—sit down!'

Awkwardly, Stephanie perched herself on the edge of a large burgundy-coloured leather chair and looked around the room. It was furnished beautifully, very comfortable, very vivid. She had no idea that her father had such perfect taste. The walls were a pale biscuit colour, complemented by the thick carpet scattered with dark African tribal rugs. The furniture was a mixture of brilliantly designed modern and antiques, with glass shelves near the long windows holding a vast collection of carved and painted birds.

'This is a lovely room,' she said shyly, her eye caught by the birds as she tried for some kind of communication with her half-sister.

Carina's glance was bored, satisfied. 'Yes, I've become very fond of this house. The only pity is that it's so far from London—lovely for weekends, though.'

'You have a house in London too?' It was a shock to realise just how little she knew about Carina. It was a shock to realise that they were actually related.

'I have a small flat,' Carina corrected coolly. 'Father sold the house years ago, didn't you know?'

'No, I didn't know.' Stephanie could still remember the house where she had spent her childhood, the wild rambling garden, the huge old rooms. If she had time while she was here, perhaps she would go and see it again.

'I wish we'd kept in touch,' she said impulsively.

'We never did get on very well,' Carina reminded her with a slight smile.

'No . . . No, I know, but we were only children. I hope we'll be friends now.'

Carina laughed, not unkindly, and shook her shining head. 'It depends on what you mean by friendship,' she said drily.

Before Stephanie could answer, Wayne appeared with a tray, kicking open the door. Carina frowned at him, but he only smiled cheerfully. 'Rose is in one of her moods, so I made the coffee myself.' He set down the tray in front of Carina. 'You can pour, my dear,' he told her, his mouth curved with amusement. 'She also wants to know what time you'll be wanting dinner.'

'That woman is impossible!' Carina exclaimed delicately, as she poured the coffee. 'Anybody would think she owned the house!'

'Rose loves me,' Wayne explained, pulling a smug face at Stephanie, 'but she can't stand Carina.'

Stephanie couldn't help smiling as she gratefully sipped the hot coffee. She couldn't believe that Carina and Wayne were romantically involved with each other. They seemed to have a sort of love-hate, brother-sister relationship. Had Carina been more approachable, she would have asked. But as it was, she did not dare.

'Coffee finished?' Carina rose. 'I'll show you to your room. I'm sure you'll want to freshen up before dinner.'

'Yes, thank you.' Stephanie stood up, still feeling awkward.

'Want me to carry your case?' Wayne looked up from his perusal of the evening newspaper.

She smiled. 'No, I can manage, thanks.'

She followed Carina up the thickly carpeted stairs, down a long terracotta-coloured corridor to her room.

'I hope you'll be comfortable here.' Carina was coolly polite as she pushed open the door and went in. Stephanie followed, gasping with delight as she looked round. It was an enormous room, with long windows. The bed was huge, a dark four-poster, draped and covered in pure white, the furniture dark, the walls and carpets pale. 'It's beautiful—thank you.'

'Don't thank me,' Carina said carelessly. 'Come down to the lounge when you're ready and we'll have dinner. There'll be just the three of us tonight.'

She had gone before Stephanie had a chance to say anything else. She shrugged and pulled her suitcase up on to the bed. She wasn't quite sure what she had expected from Carina, from the house, but things weren't as bad as she had feared they might be. Her half-sister was quite friendly in a dismissive way, and the house was very beautiful.

She wandered into the connecting bathroom, delighted with the luxury of the dark tiled shower, oval bath and gold taps. It had been a long tiring journey and the thought of a hot shower before dinner was very welcoming.

She quickly unpacked her case and walking to the windows, pushed aside the drifting lace curtains and stared out into the night. It was pitch black, the moon rising over the sea. The view was infinite, mysterious, beautiful. She had always loved the sea, drawn to it by instincts she did not fully understand. She turned away, smiling at her fanciful thoughts, and looked through the clothes she had brought with her, needing something suitable for dinner.

She finally chose a soft flowing dress of patterned silk crêpe-de-chine, its autumn colours bringing out the beauty of her hair. She showered and made up her face, then pinned back her hair in a neat chignon before dressing. That was better, she thought, as she examined her reflection in the mirror. She looked poised and sophisticated, and the knowledge gave her self-confidence a boost. Carina's disparaging glances at her jeans and wild loose hair had left her feeling scruffy and inferior and decidedly awkward.

She left her room and made her way back downstairs to the lounge. There was music playing and the fire was still roaring. Carina was flicking through a magazine, while Wayne, now changed into a dark dinner jacket, was pouring drinks.

'What will you have?' he asked as she entered the room, his eyes sliding appreciatively over her from head to toe.

'Sherry—dry, please.' She smiled at him and moved across the room towards the fire.

Carina looked up from her magazine, took in Stephanie's appearance, then lowered her eyes again without a word. Stephanie took a cigarette from Wayne and chatted to him until they went in to dinner.

The meal was delicious and Stephanie found herself eating heartily. She also met Rose, a thin, strong-looking woman in her sixties, with piercing eyes, a gruff manner, and, as Wayne had said, a great affection for him. Carina was mostly silent throughout the meal, her conversation mostly dismissive, mostly aimed at Wayne.

Stephanie watched them with interest. Wayne seemed totally unconcerned by Carina's cutting remarks, even when she was rather nasty with him. He was extra-friendly to Stephanie, trying perhaps, to make up for Carina's coldness.

'Stephanie's engaged, you know?' he commented to Carina over dessert.

'Really?' Carina's pale eyes suddenly fixed on the sapphire engagement ring on Stephanie's finger. 'When's the wedding?'

Luke Baroda's confident words pushed their way into Stephanie's mind unbidden: 'You won't marry Sangster.' She shivered, despite the heat.

'The date ... the date isn't fixed yet,' she said, flushing under Carina's suddenly interested gaze.

'Is the reluctance on your part or on his?' Carina's mouth curved into a smile and Stephanie's colour rose higher.

'Neither. . . .' As soon as she said it, she knew she

was lying. She had been reluctant to name the wedding day. Dean had already recognised that reluctance and was becoming increasingly impatient. She couldn't explain it to him—it was just that something inside her was holding back. It was totally unreasonable, inexplicable, but strong enough for her to take notice of.

'Don't let Carina bully you,' Wayne cut in cheerfully. 'She's only jealous. The man she wants is displaying the kind of reluctance that not even Carina, with all her charm, can break. Isn't that so, darling?'

'Do be quiet, Wayne, and don't be so bloody childish.' Carina's voice was calmly controlled, yet her eyes glittered with sudden anger.

Wayne raised his eyebrows. 'You see?' he said triumphantly to Stephanie. 'Not even gracious in defeat!'

'Wayne . . .!' The warning was clear.

'Okay, okay, I know when I'm beaten.' He bent his head to his wine, his eyes still glinting with amusement, and Stephanie avoided looking at Carina, feeling an outsider to their strange games.

She was drooping with tiredness as they sat in the lounge again later, sipping brandy. The long journey was taking its toll.

Carina was talking on the telephone, her voice light, filled with warmth and laughter. Wayne was chatting to Stephanie, and she stared into the firelight, jumping as she heard him say,

'Don't you agree?'

'I'm sorry, Wayne, I'm afraid I wasn't listening. I'm falling asleep,' she explained apologetically. 'If you'll excuse me, I think I'll go to bed.'

Carina was replacing the receiver as she spoke, and she cut in, 'I'll telephone Father's solicitors in the morning. I'm sure you're as anxious as I am to get this business sorted out.' Then you can go home, her eyes added silently.

Stephanie nodded. 'Yes, of course. You ... you weren't very specific in your letter. Is there some trouble about the estate? Have you any idea how long it will take?'

'I think it better that the solicitors explain all the details,' said Carina, lighting a cigarette. 'I have no wish to drag it out, obviously I want it dealt with as soon as possible.'

She was not being particularly helpful, but there was nothing Stephanie could say. 'Yes ... right. Goodnight.'

As she walked slowly up the stairs to her room, she could hear Wayne's voice, but could not catch the words. He was arguing with Carina.

She shrugged tiredly. They were a strange couple. She remembered what Wayne had said over dinner about the man Carina wanted. Was that just another of his jokes? No doubt she would find out sooner or later.

She washed and slid out of her clothes, having only enough energy to crawl into bed and switch out the light. I must ring Dean, she thought, as she drifted off into sleep.

The following morning, she still felt exhausted.

Carina was drinking coffee when she entered the dining room.

'You look dreadful,' her half-sister commented bluntly. 'Didn't you sleep well?'

'I didn't sleep enough,' Stephanie replied with a smile. 'Jet-lag.'

'Well, I'm driving up to London after breakfast, I have to see my agent. I'll call in on the solicitors while I'm there and arrange an appointment. Anything I can get you?'

She was not offering Stephanie a lift, and Stephanie was rather glad. She was in no mood for the noise and the bustle of the city. 'No, I don't think so, but thanks for offering.'

She sat down and poured herself some coffee. The weather was fine but windy, she could see the trees being pulled back and forth outside the windows.

Rose bustled in with a rack of fresh toast.

'Tell Rose what you'd like for breakfast,' said Carina, looking up from the letter she was reading.

'Toast and coffee will be fine.' Stephanie smiled at the housekeeper, who merely eyed her dourly, set down the toast, checked the coffee pot and silently left the room.

Carina watched her go with narrowed eyes. 'I don't know how that woman keeps her job,' she said irritably. 'Her rudeness is appalling!'

'Has she been here long?' Stephanie rather liked the look of Rose, despite her sternness.

'Years and years, unfortunately. She dotes on the men, of course, spoils them rotten.'

Men? Stephanie frowned, about to ask, but Carina was glancing at her watch and moving elegantly to her feet.

'I'm late. I should be back some time this afternoon.' She walked out of the room without looking back, and Stephanie poured herself more coffee, feeling suddenly miserable.

It was clear that Carina had no intention of spending her time with Stephanie. In fact, she gave the strong impression that Stephanie's visit was just an inconvenience that had to be endured.

Stephanie had hoped that they might become friends, at least spend some time together, getting to know each other. Carina was, after all, her closest relative, they should have had *something* in common.

Yet they knew absolutely nothing about each other, and Carina obviously didn't care.

What had she expected, anyway? That she and Carina would act like sisters, after ten years apart? She sighed at her own naïvety and finished her coffee. Then, setting down her cup, she piled the breakfast dishes on to a tray and went in search of the kitchen.

Rose took the tray as soon as she opened the kitchen door. 'You shouldn't have bothered,' she muttered sourly.

Stephanie smiled. 'I don't mind. I'll give you a hand with the washing up if you like.'

'No need.' Rose indicated a dishwasher near the sink.

'Oh.' Stephanie turned to go. It seemed that Rose wasn't exactly friendly either.

'Gone off to London, has she? Left you to your own devices?' asked Rose, with a grim satisfaction in her voice, as though that was all one could expect.

'Carina?' Stephanie prevaricated. 'Yes, she's just left.'

'Plain as the nose on your face what that one's after!'

'Rose!'

The housekeeper's face split in a humourless grin. 'Shocked? You're her sister aren't you?' She paused for a moment, staring at Stephanie, then said, 'No, you're different. She'll never get him—you might, though.'

Convinced that Rose was totally mad, Stephanie turned and left the kitchen. She wandered through the house, unsure what to do with herself now that Carina was gone. It seemed that she was on her own until her half-sister returned.

Before she had flown over, she had had no idea that she would be left on her own. If she had imagined it all, she had imagined an immediate meeting with the solicitors and time spent with Carina before flying back to the island and Dean.

She thought of Dean now, picturing his face, creased in that charming, carefree smile, the brightness of his hair, the vivid blue of his eyes, and inexplicably her eyes filled with tears. She dashed them away with angry fingers and ran upstairs to collect her coat.

She would go for a walk and get some fresh air, some fresh thoughts. The wind was sharp and salty, yet behind it the sun was warm, as she strode along the cliffs. She stared down at the white-edged sea, crashing and breaking on the dark rocks, and let the cry of the gulls fill her mind, the harsh, salt-laden air fill her lungs.

Wayne found her hours later as she wandered back towards the house, feeling hungry. He smiled as they came face to face. 'Hi, I've been looking for you.'

'Carina's gone to London,' she told him.

'I know, she told me this morning. Been walking?'

Stephanie nodded. 'For miles. I found myself in a tiny little village and had coffee in a minute tea-shop on the sea-front.' She flicked back her windblown hair, and making a sudden decision said, 'Wayne, I've got a bit of a problem, and I wondered if you could help me.'

'Fire away.' He turned to look at her, his eyes alive with interest.

'Well . . . it's rather awkward, but the thing is that Carina's letter came totally out of the blue. You see, after my parents were divorced, my mother and I left England and I've had no contact with Carina for the ten years since then. I don't even know what she does for a living, and I wondered . . . well, I wondered if you could fill me in with a few details. I'd feel awfully embarrassed asking Carina.'

Wayne smiled and slid his arm around her

shoulders. 'Okay, let's see. Carina's an actress, she also does some modelling jobs on the side to make money, because acting jobs aren't exactly thick on the ground. She lives in London, as you know. And when your father was taken ill, he came here to convalesce after leaving hospital. Carina came with him, and she's been here ever since—vested interests, you might say.'

Stephanie stared at him in surprise. 'You mean—the house doesn't belong to her? It's yours?'

Wayne shook his head. 'No, I only wish it was. It belongs to my cousin. Your father worked for him, they were close friends.'

It was a surprise. Somehow, Stephanie had automatically assumed that the house had belonged to her father, and now to Carina.

'I thought . . .' she shrugged expressively.

'Well, now you know.' Wayne smiled broadly, then guided her through the gardens towards the house.

'And you and Carina . . .?' She broke off, flushing. It was rather a personal question.

'Chance would be a fine thing. No, we're not living together, if that's what you think—in fact, there is absolutely nothing going on between us.'

'Oh.' Stephanie digested this in silence. The reality of the situation was far different from what she had imagined. 'You do live here, though?'

Wayne nodded.

'I didn't realise. . . .'

'Well, it won't be for long—it's a strictly temporary arrangement. I'll be moving out before Christmas.' He looked down at Stephanie's pleated brow and laughed. 'Now you're totally confused!'

'Yes!' she admitted.

'It's a good thing I put you in the picture, then.'

'It's pretty complicated,' she said, pulling a face at him. 'You must admit.'

Wayne shrugged. 'It all seems fairly simple to me. Too much time in the sun,' he tapped her head, his eyes teasing, 'it affects the brain.'

Stephanie laughed, then noticed that he was staring at a long silver grey car parked outside the front door.

'Visitors?' she queried.

He shook his head. 'Prepare to meet the object of Carina's unrequited affections.'

'What?'

She followed him into the house, laughing, then stopped dead in her tracks in the high hall, as she came face to face with Luke Baroda.

CHAPTER THREE

SHE felt a sick fear cramping her stomach as their eyes met. The object of Carina's unrequited affections, Wayne had said. Her mind couldn't cope with the enormity of the coincidence. Wayne was talking. 'Stephanie, let me introduce my cousin, Luke Baroda—Luke, Stephanie Maxwell.'

Cousin. The owner of the house. Wayne's boss. She stared into Luke Baroda's narrowed green eyes, speechless with shock.

'Miss Maxwell and I have already met,' he said coolly, his glance sliding over her tousled, windswept hair, the healthy glow in her cheeks. He was obviously not in the least surprised to see her.

Wayne's eyebrows rose. 'You didn't tell me,' he accused her.

'I ... I didn't know. I didn't realise. . . .' she faltered, and dragged her eyes away from Luke Baroda's slight smile.

He could see how shocked she was. He was *enjoying* her discomfort, she thought bitterly. She hated him!

Wayne was staring at her expectantly, obviously waiting for some sort of explanation—explanation that she was totally incapable of providing. She couldn't even think straight, but she did know that everything suddenly fitted—all those stray remarks made by Carina, by Rose and Wayne, that had struck a chord of incongruity.

Paranoid thoughts were shooting round her brain. Perhaps it had all been planned. Luke Baroda was a powerful man, even more dangerous on his home

ground. She looked at him and her stomach turned
over. He was wearing a dark suit, expensive,
beautifully cut. His black hair was neatly brushed. She
saw his power, his wealth, his self-assurance, and felt
threatened.

'You look as though you've seen a ghost.' Wayne
was clearly intrigued as he took her arm. 'Let's find
some coffee.' He turned to his cousin. 'Luke?'

'I have a couple of calls to make.'

Stephanie heard Luke's low voice with a shiver of
awareness, knowing that he was watching her.

'Another successful trip?'

Luke nodded, his mouth curved in a hard smile.

Still in a state of shock, Stephanie allowed herself to
be led into the lounge. She sat by the fire, her body
numb, not even noticing Rose appearing with a tray
piled high with coffee and sandwiches.

She was stunned by the realisation that without her
knowing it, Luke Baroda was already intertwined in
the fabric of her life. He was connected with her
father, with Dean and Carina and Wayne. She was
overawed by the fatefulness of it all.

And he knew that. His knowledge and wisdom
scared the living daylights out of her. She felt as
though she was in a long dark tunnel. Luke Baroda
could provide the light if she dared to ask for it. She
didn't dare.

'Well, you *are* a dark horse!' Wayne handed her a
cup of steaming aromatic coffee. 'When did you meet
him?'

For a moment, in her confusion, he seemed
unnaturally curious. 'Does it matter?' she asked rather
sharply.

'Not if you don't want to tell me.'

His tone was offended, and she was immediately
contrite.

'I'm sorry, Wayne, it was a bit of a shock, that's all.' What an understatement! she thought hysterically. 'I had no idea he was your cousin. I met him at home, he was playing the tables at the casino . . .'

She tried to make her voice sound casual, normal, but didn't succeed very well.

Fortunately, Wayne didn't ask any more questions, and they sat in fairly companionable silence until the door opened and Stephanie knew without turning round that Luke had just entered the room.

He moved silently, and she almost jumped out of her skin as he came into her line of vision, coiling his powerful body into a chair opposite hers.

He and Wayne were talking, but Stephanie didn't hear a word. Her fingers were clenched tightly round her coffee cup and she kept her head down, intimidated by his presence.

He must have known, she thought angrily. He must have known the moment we met who I was. He had been playing games with her!

She got to her feet, her body stiff with a flaring outrage that she knew she would not be able to control if she stayed. Luke was watching her intently and she felt the colour pouring into her cheeks.

'Excuse me. . . .' She fled the room, her anger burning in her downturned face. Luke's narrowed eyes followed her to the door.

She paused in the hall, restless and furious, not knowing what to do. She would ring Dean, there was a telephone in the dining room. She needed some reassurance. As she moved towards the door, she heard Luke laughing, deep amused laughter that raised the hair on the back of her neck. She shut herself in the dining room with a bang, took a cigarette from a box on the table and lit it with ridiculously shaking hands. She knew a desperate urge to get out of the house, out of England.

Stephanie dialled the casino, and Camil answered from Dean's office. 'The boss is on the other phone,' he told her, a smile in his faintly-accented voice.

'How are you?' she asked in bright friendly tones.

Camil was an islander of French ancestry. He was Dean's right-hand man. Stephanie liked him, had known him for years, and they chatted until Dean came on the line.

'How's it going, honey?' His light, familiar voice somehow reassured her.

'Slowly,' she answered with a sigh. 'Carina hasn't arranged the meeting with the solicitors yet.'

'You sound pretty low—what's the matter?'

'I miss you,' she admitted softly. 'I want to come home.'

'It won't take long, honey, you'll be back before you know it.' He sounded very far away, placating her as though she was a whining child, a slight preoccupation in his voice.

'I know, and I'm sorry for moaning so much.' She paused, then said quietly, 'Luke Baroda's here.'

Dean's attention snapped on to her. She could almost hear him sitting up and taking notice. '*What?*'

'Luke Baroda. He's a friend of Carina's. This house belongs to him,' she explained dully. 'Dean, I. . . .'

She didn't get the chance to finish.

'Hell, that's incredible!' He sounded very pleased, excited.

'Yes, isn't it. Dean. . . .'

'You're actually staying in the same house?'

'*Yes.*' She wanted to talk seriously.

'Stephanie, honey, do me a favour—be nice to him, huh?'

'But I don't like him,' she protested, shocked by the very suggestion.

Dean's voice was sharp with irritation. 'What does that matter? I'm not asking you to sleep with him—just be nice, be friendly. I hear that Luke Baroda is not immune to a pretty face.'

'*Dean!*' She could hardly believe her ears. What he was suggesting was not only distasteful, but verging on the immoral. 'I couldn't, I just *couldn't*!' she said fiercely.

'Stephanie, listen to me, baby.' The voice on the other end of the line was soft now, and persuasive. 'Luke Baroda could do me—and you—a lot of good. He's bought a hotel on the other side of the island and I want a casino in that hotel. Don't you see? If I could get even a toe-hold in Baroda's organisation, we would be set up for life. I'm not asking you to do this purely for me, it's for both of us.'

She listened to his rapid words with a sinking heart. It was against her nature to pretend a liking for somebody she positively hated. Luke Baroda was not a man easily fooled. He was clever, astute and perceptive. She had the uneasy feeling that he could probably read her mind—she wouldn't be able to hide anything from him; she was sure of that.

'Dean, I don't think it would work—I don't like him,' she said urgently, trying to make him see how she hated the idea.

'Whether or not you like him is irrelevant. Listen, how long do you expect this legal business to take?'

'I've no idea—why?'

'Can't you take a guess?' His voice told her that his brain was ticking away, calculating, formulating plans.

'A week or two, perhaps, but I really can't say. Why?' she asked again.

'I'm thinking of flying over. I miss you.' Dean laughed. 'Do you think Carina would swallow that? It's perfectly natural for me to want to be with my fiancée, after all.'

As he spoke, Stephanie felt a dull depression settling over her. Was this all he could think about—business? She had asked him to come with her and he had refused. Now, only because Luke Baroda was here, he would come. She felt a rush of hot tears filling her eyes.

'Do you really want to see me?' she asked sadly.

Dean groaned. 'Don't be silly, honey, of course I do. I love you.'

She clung to the words desperately. She was being unfair. She couldn't blame him for being ambitious, it was an inherent part of his character—she knew that. She also knew that he meant no harm to her.

'When will you come?' she asked shakily.

'As soon as I can. Tell Carina.'

They chatted for a few moments longer, Dean making a big effort to reassure her, perhaps sensing that he had shocked her. But it made no particular difference. She still felt miserable as she hung up. She had felt so alone before telephoning him, lonely and uncared for in this house of strangers. Dean had been unable to comfort her.

Their relationship had never been tested before, she realised. Life on Moahu was so easy, so problem-free. There had never been any serious disagreements between them. The nearest they had come to arguing had been over the wedding date. In every other instance Stephanie had given in to Dean, sure that, despite her own misgivings, he was right. She had grown up with him, he had been almost like an older brother, revered, respected. He had always known better because he was older and wiser and stronger. She supposed her life had been carefully sheltered; Dean was the only man she had ever known. His charm had carried her away.

But now she was growing up, an adult instead of an

indulged child, doubts were constantly creeping into her mind, and this business over Luke Baroda created the biggest doubt of all. How *could* Dean suggest she be nice to him?

She wandered around the dining room, smoking another cigarette and trying to think rationally. Would she have been so appalled by the idea if Luke Baroda had been short and bald and sixty? Somehow she doubted it. It was the man himself who produced her shock. She had no idea how Luke Baroda would react if she started being 'nice' to him. He had said he wanted her. She shivered involuntarily, unwilling to even think about that, and stubbing out her cigarette, wandered into the hall.

I must remember to pay Carina for the phone call, she thought, staring up at the patterned ceiling.

She had nothing to do until dinner. She was at a completely loose end, a situation that Carina had forced upon her.

She heard Luke and Wayne talking through the lounge door, and stepped away, jumping as the door opened, shooting out of the front door into the garden, without looking back. As she walked towards the sea again, she decided that tomorrow, she would put her time to good use. She had not expected to be left on her own by the one person she knew in England, but if Carina wanted it that way, Stephanie would fend for herself.

Her chin lifted determinedly as she climbed down a steep rocky path towards the tiny bay. The weather was cold now, the wind still high. She listened to the gulls and walked to the water's edge, watching a tiny crab scuttling across the wet sand.

It was beautiful here, she thought, almost happily, her good spirits returning. There was a wildness, a stormy darkness that Moahu lacked. There, the ocean was calm and crystal clear, everything was bright and vivid and hot. She stared out towards the overcast horizon, where the dull blue sky met the grey sea. It was empty.

The wind lifted her golden hair, whipping it around her head. She stood at the foaming edge of the sea, letting the cold salt water wet her ankles, and her loneliness suddenly made her feel happy. It was good for her, it would teach her about herself.

She wanted to paint this scene, this tiny unfriendly bay. Tomorrow she would go to the nearest town and buy some paints, some paper.

She turned back towards the cliffs and saw Luke Baroda standing only feet away, watching her. Strangely, she was not surprised. He had to be here. His suit was gone. He wore jeans, old and faded, that clung to his lean hips and strong legs, and a black sweater that lent a saturnine darkness to his hard face. He was smoking, the smoke drifting from his nostrils and lips, whipped away by the dancing wind.

She could read no expression in his face or his narrowed eyes as they stared at each other, but she felt that she was at his mercy on this deserted beach. Ridiculous, she told herself sternly. But the silence between them seemed to build up into a tension that she had to break.

'Did you follow me?' she asked in a small voice.

He moved closer with smooth cat-like grace, as though her words were an invitation. He towered over her, well over six foot tall, his narrowed gaze sliding with slow insolence over her face, her body.

'Yes,' he admitted casually, 'I followed you.'

Stephanie licked her suddenly dry lips, her eyes veering away from his, resting on the hard, sensual line of his mouth. His direct honesty floored her.

'Why?' she demanded huskily.

Luke smiled. Their eyes met again and her heart turned over violently.

'It can be dangerous along here. I saw you leaving the house.'

'I can look after myself,' she muttered, fighting the overpowering pull of his charm, his magnetism.

His dark brows rose, clearly cynical. 'Can you? You're wandering around like a lost child!'

Stephanie bit her lip absently. She knew that all too well, but she wasn't about to admit it to him. 'Carina . . .' she began.

'Carina doesn't give a damn,' he cut in, cruel and brutally direct. 'She doesn't even want you here, you know that.'

'Why are you so cruel?' Her voice was shaky, her eyes suddenly brilliant with unshed tears.

Luke frowned. He had not realised that she was so very vulnerable. He stared down at the soft, lonely lines of her face. 'I'm sorry,' his voice was low and quiet, 'I didn't mean to hurt you.'

'You couldn't hurt me,' she retorted, hating him because he could see how defenceless she was against Carina's coldness.

'I'm glad to hear it.' A slight smile touched the corners of his mouth. 'Walk with me?'

There was an order behind the deep question, but Stephanie found herself automatically obeying, falling into step beside him. He matched his pace with hers and she stared across the water, as they walked the windswept sand, never looking at him but fiercely aware of his presence.

'How do you like England? Wayne tells me you were only a child when you left.'

He was being polite. It was an ordinary friendly question but defensive distrust flared inside her.

'I like it,' she replied shortly, then thought of Dean,

and added, 'This coastline is beautiful, so different from home—wild and stormy. . . .' She broke off, averting her face. Luke wouldn't want to know.

'You wouldn't like to live here, though?' Again there was an impersonal coolness in the question.

Stephanie shrugged, glancing at the hard lines of his profile. 'I don't know—the question won't really arise.' She felt the need to remind him, and perhaps herself, of Dean. 'When we get married, we'll stay where Dean's work is.'

Luke nodded, his expression unreadable. 'Still no date fixed?'

'No.' She stopped walking, pretending interest in a tiny rock pool, staring into its sandy depth, her mouth a fierce straight line.

'You don't seem in any mad hurry,' he remarked, watching her.

Her angry eyes met the veiled depths of his for a second, before veering away again. 'Is there any reason why we should be?' she demanded defensively.

His slow smile gave her an answer that brought the colour pouring into her cheeks. She remembered his promise the night he had driven her back from the casino and knew that he was remembering it too. 'It's none of your business, anyway,' she said angrily, and walked away.

Luke caught her arm before she had taken two paces, moving quickly and silently. She looked at his tanned hand, fingers curling round her arm.

'You do have a bad temper,' he commented with a mild smile.

'Because I object to your personal questions?' Stephanie retorted.

'If you were sure, they wouldn't upset you,' he replied coolly.

'I *am* sure,' she said through clenched teeth, and

knew again that she was lying.

'If you say so.' He didn't believe a word.

'I do.'

She moved her arm and his restraining hand dropped. As she walked on, not looking at him, her thoughts were in chaos. She didn't need him to reinforce her own doubts. Yet he seemed to take a personal pleasure in doing so, had done so right from the moment of their meeting.

'You knew who I was when we first met,' she suddenly accused him. 'Didn't you?'

'Before we met,' he acknowledge softly.

'Before? But how . . .? I'd never heard of you!'

'Your father showed me a photograph,' he explained briefly.

Stephanie stared at him in amazement. She had not seen her father for ten years. How could he have had photographs of her? Luke surely wouldn't have recognised her as a child.

'A recent photograph?'

'Taken last year, I believe.' All the time he was speaking, he was staring at her with a cool, probing intensity, his expression blank, his eyes veiled.

She couldn't really understand what he was saying. 'How could he have got hold of a photograph?' she wondered, half to herself.

Luke shrugged his powerful shoulders. If he knew, he clearly had no intenton of telling her.

'It *was* a coincidence, wasn't it, us meeting at the casino?' She felt very unsure of herself. There was something strange about this whole business. She got the impression that he was testing her.

'What do you think?'

'I think it was—you were on business.'

'Yes,' he agreed expressionlessly.

'You didn't say anything, though. . . .'

'You weren't exactly ready to listen to anything I had to say,' he reminded her with amusement.

'It is amazing, you must admit,' she said thoughtfully, convinced that there was more to it than he was telling.

'Paranoia, my child?' He was laughing at her. Stephanie ignored him.

'Carina said my father worked for you,' she said, turning to him, tilting back her golden head to look unguardedly into his face. Her heart began to race at something indefinable in his eyes.

He nodded. 'Yes. What do you want to know?'

She shrugged. 'I don't know. Everything—nothing. I didn't know him at all, you see. I wrote, but, . . .' she bit her lip, her face vulnerable, unsure.

Luke stared down at her, then reached out his hand, gently touching her cheek.

She felt the light touch of his finger as though it was flame, but was held perfectly still, caught by the sheer force of his attraction. 'Your father was basically a good man,' he told her quietly. 'He cared for you, he always held you dear, thought of you right up until the time he died.'

'Did he?' Her eyes were bright with a painful happiness.

'Yes. He was proud and as stubborn as the devil himself, but he loved you—believe that, and remember it.' He smiled then, a smile that lit the heavy green depths of his eyes, that etched deep lines in his tanned skin, a smile that caught Stephanie's breath with its potent charm.

And she smiled back involuntarily—the first time she had ever smiled at him. And in that instant, something started to grow between them, something fragile and inexplicable, but so powerful that she could feel it in every fibre of her body. She looked at him

and saw a gentleness in his eyes that made her heart
lurch. She trusted him—trusted him, yet still feared
him for his strength, his power.

'I will remember, and—thank you.' She tore her
eyes away from his, walking on legs that were
strangely weak.

'The pleasure is all mine.' There was a mocking
amusement in his voice.

Flustered, Stephanie bowed her head, acknowledg-
ing the danger of him, her heart beating too heavily.

They walked on in silence, though she could still
feel the probe of his eyes on her downturned head.
Then suddenly, he said very coolly, 'I thought
Sangster would be with you.'

She flushed, and Luke did not miss the hurt in her
eyes, the vulnerable sadness of her mouth.

'It's a very busy time,' she said stiffly. Luke's dark
brows rose, but he said nothing. 'I spoke to him on the
telephone today,' she added, and realised that she
shouldn't have told him.

'Don't tell me—he'll be flying over as soon as he
can,' said Luke, in a hard taunting voice.

'How did you . . .?' She bit her lip, aware that she
had fallen into his trap.

His mouth twisted cynically. 'It wasn't difficult to
guess.'

'You think you know everything, don't you?' she
flung at him, angry now, because somehow he could
see through Dean's every move.

'I keep my eyes open,' he agreed, pinning her with
his cool gaze. 'Which is more than can be said for
you.'

'And what is that supposed to mean?' she demanded
icily, her doubts crowding in on her as she turned on
him, her blue eyes brilliant with rage.

'You know damn well what it means!' Luke bit out

coldly. 'You're not stupid, Stephanie, you know what sort of a man Sangster is, yet you choose to keep your eyes firmly shut, wandering around like a dreaming adolescent. Well, that's fine—but you can't expect everybody else to do the same.'

'I don't know what you're talking about,' she snapped back, honestly confused.

Luke's eyes narrowed, as hard as ice beneath their heavy lids.

'Shall I tell you what his instructions were?' he taunted cynically. Stephanie glared at him in silence, and he continued, 'He'll have told you to soften me up, to use your charm on me until he arrives.' He saw her shocked astonishment and laughed humourlessly. 'So come on, my love, show me how charming you can be.' There was a liquid softness in his voice that dried her mouth and made her throat ache with tension. She couldn't find her voice. Luke took hold of her left hand, staring at the sapphire ring, the emblem of Dean's possession.

'How far will you go, I wonder, to keep your fiancé happy?'

Stephanie wrenched her hand out of his, as though he was burning her. 'Go to hell!' she muttered, in a voice that shook violently. 'Just leave me alone!'

She walked quickly away from him, her body stiff with outrage, her mind exploding with anger. How dared he? *How dared he?*

'I'm not asking you to sleep with him,' Dean had said. God, it was almost funny!

She reached the narrow cliff path, tripping in her haste to get away from him, but he was right behind her.

'*Go away!*' she hissed over her shoulder, as she tried to struggle to her feet.

His hand closed urgently on her arm, pulling her

up, whirling her round to face him. His mouth was a hard, angry line, his eyes glittering dangerously.

'You crazy little fool!' he snapped harshly, his fingers bruising her skin through the clothes she wore. 'Calm down, for God's sake!'

'Calm down?' Stephanie repeated incredulously. '*Calm down?* It may interest you to know, Mr Baroda, that I wouldn't try to charm you if you were the last man on earth! Dean might be a swine for suggesting it, but you . . . you're even more of a swine for trying to take advantage of the fact that he did!' She paused for breath, then added furiously, 'I don't want you, I don't even like you. I hate you!'

There was a moment of explosive silence as they stared into each other's eyes, then Luke reached for her and dragged her against the lean strength of his body, one hand sliding up the length of her spine, to tangle in her silken hair and bring back her head.

His own head seemed to lower in slow motion, his mouth brushing hers unhurriedly, over and over, until he groaned deep in his throat, his lips parting hers, and began kissing her with a hungry demand that made her legs give way beneath her.

She would have fallen had he not been holding her so tightly. She was too shocked to struggle or fight him. She felt the touch of his mouth almost with wonder, and without her wanting it, she felt a deep response triggering inside her, as an urgent primaeval passion flared between them. Of their own volition, her arms crept around his neck, her fingers tangling in the vital blackness of his hair.

She could not help her response—her lips moved innocently under the fierce pressure of Luke's, the kiss still deepening, blocking out everything else until she knew only the heated pleasure of his mouth, and the hot excitement inside herself.

After endless moments, Luke reluctantly raised his head and stared down at her flushed face and swollen lips, through eyes glittering with desire.

'Stephanie. . . .' He said her name quietly, the word stolen by the wind.

She stared back into the hard planes of his face, trembling, her thoughts in turmoil, lifting her hand up and touching the bruised softness of her lips. She had never before been kissed like that. She was dazed by the unbidden violence of her own response.

Sensing her dazed state, Luke took her hand without a word, and together they climbed the rocky path back to the house. Stephanie's mind was completely blank. She felt the immense strength in the hand that engulfed hers. She was desperately aware of him beside her, moving with sure easy grace. He knew what he was doing.

And as the spell of that kiss began to fade, her eyes filled with tears. She felt raw, defenceless and very guilty. She thought of Dean and of what she had just done, and pulling her hand out of Luke's, ran away towards the house, not stopping until she was in her room, leaning weakly on the closed door.

Something had happened down by the sea, something she did not yet have the courage to face. But she did know one thing for certain: Luke Baroda had the power to destroy her.

CHAPTER FOUR

SHE dressed carelessly for dinner, her mind running over and over the day's events. Luke Baroda had only arrived that morning—incredible! It seemed as though he had been at the house for years.

The day ran back for ever—Dean's phone call, finding out from Wayne that the house did not belong to Carina, the incident on the beach. And she still had dinner to face. Heaven only knew what new surprises were waiting.

Emotionally, she felt exhausted, as she slid into a dress of pale blue cashmere. Whatever Carina said about the weather, Stephanie was finding it rather cold. She checked her make-up, brushed her newly-washed hair, then sat down on the bed, unwilling to go downstairs.

She didn't feel at all hungry and she felt no inclination to face Luke Baroda after this afternoon. She rested her head in her hands and sighed. A week ago she had been so happy in the pattern of her life. Everything had been so simple.

Her eye caught the clock on the bedside table. It was time to go downstairs. At least Carina and Wayne would be at dinner; that was some consolation. She left her room and strolled down the richly-carpeted stairs, viewing her surroundings with more interest, now she knew who they belonged to. The house was very old, filled with charm, yet it had been extensively modernised. The rooms were filled with lovingly cared for wood—nothing of the old house had been destroyed, it was filled with paintings and carvings and beautiful fabrics from around the world.

Two huge modern abstract paintings lined the wall behind the stairs, their violent colours reflected serenely in the surrounding decor. All around the house she could see rare examples of fine art. priceless antiques, beautiful furniture. Luke was a man of perfect taste and wide knowledge.

The telephone was ringing as she reached the hall, and she hovered, unsure whether to answer it. Nobody appeared, and she finally picked up the receiver.

It was Carina. 'Stephanie?' Her cool voice sounded impatient.

'Yes, where are——?' She didn't get time to finish the question.

'I shan't be back tonight, I'm staying in London. Tell Wayne, will you, darling?'

'Yes, of course. Carina——' Stephanie wanted to ask about the solicitors. As soon as her father's estate was sorted out, she would be able to leave here and, she hoped, never see Luke Baroda again.

'I don't have time to talk now,' Carina cut in. 'I'll see you tomorrow.' And before Stephanie could say another word, before she could even tell Carina that Luke Baroda was back, the phone was hung up.

Stephanie stared at the receiver in her hand for a moment, then replaced it. She would have to wait until tomorrow for news from the solicitors. She walked into the lounge, hoping Wayne would be there. He wasn't. Luke sat alone by the open fire, reading a newspaper. Angrily, Stephanie felt her heart beating faster as she looked at him. He was wearing a black velvet dinner jacket that emphasised the width of his shoulders, his white shirt startling against the tanned skin at his throat and wrists. His hair was neatly brushed and still faintly damp.

He looked up as she entered and put aside the

newspaper. His dark eyes slid over her as she stood so tense and slender in pale blue wool, the soft light turning her hair into a halo of spun gold.

He moved indolently to his feet. 'Can I get you a drink?' he asked with urbane politeness.

'Martini, please, with ice.' Her voice sounded shaky even though she strove to keep it normal. She watched him pour two drinks, watched his strong brown hands curling around the crystal glasses. He had beautiful hands, she thought with wonder.

He carried the glasses back to the fire. 'Sit down,' he said, smiling. Stephanie moved nervously across the room and sank into a huge leather chair. Luke handed her the Martini and she jumped as their fingers accidentally brushed. He saw her reaction, and his green eyes became faintly mocking as he sat down opposite to her.

'Carina telephoned,' she told him, staring down into her glass and absently noticing that her hand was trembling. 'She's staying in London tonight.'

Luke smiled, unsurprised. 'Wayne won't be in until late either, so there'll just be the two of us for dinner,' he drawled softly.

Stephanie's heart sank deep into her stomach. The very thought horrified her. How could she cope with this powerful, disturbing man? She couldn't think of a word to say to him. Usually she could chat lightly to people she hardly knew, even people she did not particularly like, but Luke Baroda was in a class of his own. He mocked her attempts at small talk, he watched her in a way that made her very uneasy.

He did not seem to care that Carina would not be back. Was her half-sister in love with him? Would she have come back from London had she known he was here? Somehow Stephanie thought she would. And how did Luke feel about Carina? He gave

absolutely nothing away. Wayne had said that Carina's
feelings were not reciprocated.

It was none of her business anyway, she decided,
and sipped her Martini.

'Is . . . is Wayne out on business?' she asked, after a
few moments of unbearable silence.

'I don't think so,' Luke replied with a faint smile. 'I
believe he's gone out to dinner with a friend.'

'Oh, I see.' Stephanie finished her drink and placed
her glass carefully on a small table. The atmosphere
was tense, almost threatening. There must be some
way I can get out of this, she thought desperately. But
at that moment Rose appeared and announced that
dinner was ready. Stephanie watched her smiling at
Luke and almost laughed. Carina was in for a tough
time if she married him. Rose definitely knew who she
liked, and Carina wasn't one of that number!

She walked slowly into the dining room, Luke right
behind her. The table was set for three.

'Carina won't be eating,' Luke told Rose.

The housekeeper raised her eyebrows, looked at
Stephanie and smiled thinly. Without knowing why,
Stephanie felt herself flushing and was irritated by the
satisfied look in Rose's eyes. What a rude old woman!
she thought furiously, as she sat down.

The meal, though, was delicious. Whatever else
Rose was, she was a superb cook, and although
Stephanie's appetite was small, she found herself
tasting the food with delight.

Watching Luke between mouthfuls, she suddenly
wondered what sort of man he was, and suddenly
knew a deep curiosity about him. She actually knew
very little about him. He was a property tycoon, he
always won when he gambled. He was devastatingly
attractive, rich, cynical, gentle, strong—so many
things. She wondered if she had the courage to ask

him about himself. She lifted a forkful of tender beef to her mouth and decided that she probably didn't.

He was watching her too, she realised, his eyes coolly assessing. She lowered her head, her cheeks hot, aware of the soft intimacy of this dinner for two.

'You're related to Sangster, I believe,' he remarked suddenly in an expressionless voice.

Stephanie wondered how on earth he knew, and as always when Dean's name was mentioned, she felt herself prickling defensively. Guilt, perhaps, she thought cynically.

'We are distantly related,' she replied stiffly.

'Oh?' He was obviously going to push the point, she thought irritably.

'Yes, he's part of my mother's family.'

'You've known him for years, then?' he probed coolly.

'I met him when we first moved—after the divorce.' She had been lonely when they had first left England. Dean had befriended her, looked after her. It had always been like that, and Luke read as much in her faraway blue eyes.

'And what about you, Mr Baroda?' she put in quickly, anxious to divert the conversation from herself. 'Are you married?'

'You know very well that I'm not,' he replied, his eyes telling her that he knew what she was trying to do.

'No plans to?' She glanced at him from beneath her lashes.

'Maybe.' He was mocking, deliberately noncommittal.

Silenced, Stephanie ate a little more food, drank more of the light, strong wine and thought about his answer. Was he thinking of marrying Carina. For some reason, the thought jarred.

Rose bustled in and out, clearing the table after each course, tutting at Stephanie's half-clean plates.

'I think she's annoyed with me,' Stephanie said to Luke, as Rose closed the door with a snap.

He smiled. 'It's nothing personal. Rose dislikes food going to waste, she mistrusts anybody who doesn't have a hearty appetite.'

Stephanie laughed. 'I suppose that explains it. Carina said she's been here for years.'

'I inherited her from the previous owners of the house,' Luke told her drily, as he refilled her glass.

'Oh, this isn't a family house, then?' Her curiosity about him was growing. His charm pulled her strongly, even against her will.

'I have no close family, my parents died when I was young. I bought this house about ten years ago.'

Which would have been when he was in his mid-twenties, Stephanie estimated.

'Why don't you live in London?' She asked next.

Luke shrugged, drawing her eyes to the powerful strength of his shoulders. 'I have a flat in London, but I prefer to live here when I'm in England. It's almost as convenient and very much more pleasant.' There was a gently mocking amusement in his eyes as he answered her questions, and she blushed as she saw it. She was being rather nosy.

'I'm sorry, I'm being rather rude.'

'Not at all, I'm flattered by your interest—but I think it must be my turn now. Tell me about yourself.' It was an order, softened only by the charm in his eyes, the indulgence in the line of his mouth.

'You seem to know everything about me already,' she complained with an innocent smile.

Luke's brows rose, his mouth suddenly hard. 'I don't know why you're engaged to Sangster,' he said harshly.

'I love Dean,' she replied, hurt by his flaring answer.

'Love?' His voice was unbearably cynical. 'What the hell can you know of love?'

'I know enough!' she cried, that awful insidious doubt creeping over her again. 'I love him.'

'As a brother, perhaps, not as a husband.' His voice was level again, calm, certain.

Stephanie's eyes flashed anger at him. 'Why do you persist in this?' she demanded fiercely. 'Why do you keep on asking about Dean? Why do you involve yourself in something that has nothing to do with you?'

'You know why.' He smiled mockingly, his eyes holding hers so easily across the table. 'I want you, Stephanie, and I intend to have you.'

'Even though I'm engaged to somebody else? You would take me from him?' she asked in defiance.

'I'd take you from my own flesh and blood, from my closest friend—make no mistake about that,' Luke replied expressionlessly.

She was frightened by his certainty, by the toneless desire for possession in his voice.

'You're mad!' she whispered, knocking over her glass in her agitation. With horror, she watched the vivid red stain seeping into the pure white linen of the tablecloth. It seemed symbolic, and she was suddenly close to tears as the accident assumed gigantic proportions.

'Oh no!' she moaned, feverishly trying to mop up the spilled wine but only making it worse.

'Leave it,' Luke advised, his eyes softening as he watched her obvious distress. 'Rose will see to it.'

'I can't . . . I must try . . .' All at once, something seemed to snap inside her, and to her total embarrassment she found herself with her head in her

hands, crying her eyes out. Everything was too much
to cope with, and the spilled wine was the final straw.
Loneliness engulfed her, swallowing her whole.

She didn't hear Luke move, but she was too weak to
resist as he gently pulled her hands from her face,
lifting her to her feet and taking her into his arms.
Briefly she fought him, angry at her own vulnerability,
at her pathetic weakness in breaking down, but he was
too strong for her.

She looked up into his face and saw that the
possessive, tenacious hardness that had frightened her
so much had gone. His eyes were warm, gentle, and
for some reason that made her cry even more. His
arms were powerfully strong and she buried her face
against his chest, feeling the soothing stroke of his
hand through her hair.

'Oh, Stephanie,' he murmured her name quietly.
'Don't cry, nothing can be as bad as all that. I'm sorry
I was so hard on you—I don't know what drives
me . . .'

She leant against the hard warmth of his body. She
could smell the clean male scent of his skin, she could
feel the heavy muscles in the arms that held her so
tightly, and her loneliness disappeared, her tears
finally drying. When she was quiet, Luke tilted up her
face and wiped away the last tears with his thumb.

She stared up at him blindly, reading something in
his eyes that could not be translated into words or
thoughts. It suffused her whole body with warmth. He
slowly bent his black head and touched his mouth to
her forehead, his lips brushing her skin.

A violent tremor ran through her and she pulled
away from him in panic.

'You need a stiff drink,' he told her drily, so back in
the lounge, they drank coffee and brandy. Luke
switched on some music. A haunting piano filled the

room, drifting up to the high ceiling and Stephanie settled back in her chair, her mouth curved in a satisfied smile, the brandy warming her body, mingling with the wine to produce a pleasant drowsiness. She never drank much, but tonight Luke had made her so nervous, she had needed something to calm the fluttering in her stomach.

She accepted a cigarette from him, watching as he leant over to light it for her. The dim glow of the lights shadowed the harsh planes of his face, disguising the hardness of his mouth, hiding the expression in his eyes. He was so good-looking, she thought with defeated wonder, and quickly lowered her lashes in case he read that thought. Her heart jolted painfully as she looked at the tanned sheen of his cheekbones. Why did he have such an effect on her? she wondered. He could frighten her, make her laugh, comfort her and . . .

She thought of the kiss on the beach, remembered the demanding warmth of his mouth. She looked at his mouth now, firm and beautifully moulded, and almost shuddered. How could she be thinking of another man like this, when she was engaged to Dean? She closed her eyes and drew deeply on her cigarette.

It was wrong, all wrong. She *had* to fight the violently confused feelings that were growing inside her for Luke Baroda. She had seen how ruthless he was, had heard him talk with possessive cruelty.

He wanted her—that shocked her speechless. She had no idea why he wanted her. Perhaps because she belonged to someone else? Perhaps because he could not have her?

Instinct told her that an affair with Luke Baroda would leave her with a broken heart. He was an expert lover, his eyes spoke with lazy sureness of his knowledge of women. He could teach her things about life and about love, wild beautiful things, that she could not even imagine now. . . .

She stopped her thoughts short. She was crazy, thinking like that! The smile faded from her lips and she quickly finished her coffee, eager to get away. She got awkwardly to her feet as the piece of music finished.

'If . . . If you'll excuse me . . .' she began falteringly, unable to look at him. 'I think I'll get to bed.'

His eyes met hers, dark with lazy amusement. 'I won't take that as an invitation,' he murmured, and smiled as the hot colour washed up her pointed face.

Stephanie longed to be able to think of something witty and cutting to fling back at him, but her mouth was dry, her mind blank. 'Well . . . goodnight.'

'Goodnight, Stephanie.' The words were soft and deep and she had to stop herself from bolting from the room as fast as she could. She walked stiffly and slowly, not looking round, immeasurably glad when she was out of his vision.

Once in her room, though, she was restless, not tired at all, perversely wishing she had stayed in the lounge near the fire, listening to that gentle music. She showered quickly, then slid into bed, where she lay on the cool silky sheets, staring blindly into the darkness. She listened to the soothing roar of the sea, determined not to think about Luke.

Her whole life seemed to be changing. The veils were dropping from her eyes. This trip to England had awakened her. Back home, she had still been a child with a child's dreams. But something had happened here; she was not sure what it was. Still thinking hard, she drifted slowly into sleep, only to wake hours later in a cold shaking sweat. She reached for the light switch, her fingers fumbling, trembling. She pushed herself up on the pillows, not even remembering where she was for a moment, only remembering the terrifying dreams that had jolted her into wakefulness.

She stared warily round the room, half expecting to see some horrible monster crouching behind the furniture, ready to pounce. The nightmares wouldn't be expelled from her mind, and in her half-wakeful state she was still reliving them.

Struggling out of bed, she walked to the window. Outside, she could see nothing at all, the moon was hidden behind heavy clouds. The darkness alarmed her, and she ran an anxious hand through her hair and turned away.

She felt so thirsty. Looking at the clock, she saw that it was only one-thirty. Everyone would be in bed by now; she would go and make herself some tea.

She left her room cautiously and tiptoed downstairs to the kitchen, switching on the lights only when the door was closed. She crept around opening cupboards, finding what she needed, filling the kettle, then sat down at the old scrubbed table, lifting her feet off the cold tiled floor, wishing she had thought to put on some shoes. When the tea was ready, she carried it into the lounge where the embers of the fire still glowed red and warm in the darkness. She sat on the floor, knees under her chin and felt curiously happy and content. Everything would work out, she thought. She was in control of her own life.

The tea was hot and sweet. She sipped it slowly, wondering when Dean would arrive. She heard the slight noise behind her and her head whipped round in an instant. Luke stood in the doorway, the light from the hall outlining his lean body.

'Oh!' Stephanie gasped. 'I didn't realise anybody was up.'

'I had some long-distance phone calls to make,' he

replied with a slow smile, and moved into the room. She watched him with wide eyes.

'I thought you were tired,' he said, towering over her, his eyes narrowing on her lace-clad body and the wild softness of her hair.

'I had a nightmare, so I thought I'd come down and make some tea,' she explained, selfconscious under his probing gaze.

'I need something a little stronger.' He ran a hand round the back of his neck, tiredly flexing the muscles of his shoulders. He had been travelling, she remembered, watching as he poured himself a Scotch. He looked worn out. The dinner jacket was open, his tie gone, his shirt was open at the neck. In the darkness he looked big and powerful and a little threatening.

Stephanie looked away quickly as their eyes met, wishing that she had slipped on a dressing gown before leaving her room. The intimacy of their situation affected her deeply, every nerve aware of him so near. She sought for something to say to him, even though he seemed totally unconcerned by the silence between them.

'Do you know how long this legal thing will take?' she asked, her voice sounding unnaturally loud in her ears.

'Anxious to get back?' he queried, slowly swallowing his scotch.

Stephanie shrugged. 'I don't really fit in here—not that I don't appreciate you letting me stay in your house,' she added quickly.

'Carina?' he probed softly.

'I don't think we're ever going to get on. We're strangers, after all.'

'You're sisters,' he reminded her, seeing the sadness in her eyes.

'Half-sisters. *I* think that should count, but it doesn't. I can't blame Carina, though, it's nobody's fault.'

'Are you lonely here?' Luke asked gently.

'A little. Wayne and Carina are always busy. I've been hanging about all day and I don't even know when the solicitors are coming.'

Luke lit a cigarette, offering her one which she took. She watched the shadowed lines of his face in the flare of the lighter and something inside her trembled. 'It could take quite a while for your father's affairs to be sorted out,' he told her quietly.

'That's what everybody keeps saying, but nobody can tell me how long, though,' she complained, as she finished her tea.

'Stephanie, you ought to know that your father was in debt when he died,' Luke told her. 'There are a lot of legal complications.'

'In debt?' She stared at him incredulously. 'Carina didn't tell me. . . .'

'Did you expect her to?' There was a taunting mockery in the words.

'I wish I knew what was going to happen, what's going on,' she sighed miserably.

'These things take time.' His deep voice soothing her, even though she had the feeling that he knew more than he was telling her.

'I'm frightened,' she admitted, as the feeling shivered over her. 'I feel as though something awful is about to happen.'

'You may be right.' He was teasing her, but his eyes were serious, and heat exploded inside her as she read his expression.

'I'm being serious,' she said shortly, to hide the way she was feeling.

'And you don't think I am?' Luke's mouth was frankly sensual, his eyes caressing.

'Luke!' There was shock on her face, but anxiety too.

He leaned forward, his hand touching her hair. 'Nothing awful is going to happen,' he reassured her gently. 'If I knew how long it was going to take, I'd tell you. Carina has instructed them to sort out your father's affairs, and that sort of thing takes time.'

'But how did he get himself into debt?' Stephanie asked worriedly.

'He took a gamble on some investments and lost a great deal of money. It was bad luck and bad judgment,' Luke told her calmly.

Stephanie digested this carefully. It didn't allay her fears at all, but she realised that Luke couldn't tell her any more, despite the hundred and one questions buzzing in her head. It was up to the solicitors. She would have to wait until she saw them for all the details. She frowned, unable to pinpoint her feelings of foreboding.

'I suppose I'll just have to wait.'

'That's exactly what you'll have to do,' he said wryly.

She smiled at him unselfconsciously and heard the swift intake of his breath, the atmosphere changing in a second, becoming tense and mercurial. She forced her eyes away from his.

'I think I'll go back to bed now,' she said breathlessly. She wanted to run, but getting to her feet, she somehow tripped, her foot catching in the hem of her long nightdress, and would have fallen flat on her face had not Luke moved swiftly and silently. He caught her, his hands closing on her narrow waist, and lifted her back on to her feet.

Their bodies were suddenly very close. Dazed, Stephanie stared up into his face, feeling his hands against her skin, the thin lace of her gown offering no barrier to his strong touch, feeling the hard seductive warmth of him. Her heart began to beat very fast, shaking her entire body. The breath seemed trapped in her lungs as she gazed blindly into the deep green depths of his eyes.

Luke did not release her. He could feel the satin warmth of her skin beneath its thin covering. He looked down into the pale fragility of her face, and felt his whole body tensing, the muscles in his stomach tightening achingly.

Stephanie wasn't thinking straight, something impulsive and purely instinctual controlling her, as she whispered his name, shuddering as his mouth touched her forehead, before trailing a path of fire across her cheeks, her eyelids, finally parting her lips with a devastating demanding hunger. He kissed her deeply, slowly, very possessively, as though he had all the time in the world, drugging her with his passion until all coherent thought was lost to her.

She knew that she had been waiting all night for him to kiss her again, and there was nothing she could do to fight those feelings. She lifted her hands to frame his lean face, her fingers stroking the smooth tanned skin, exploring the hardness of his cheekbones. There was something dreamlike and unreal in what was happening. Luke groaned as she touched him, moulding her closer, his own hands tracing the slender curves of her body from shoulder to thigh. His heart was beating as fast as her own, she realised with shock, and a sweet ache ran warmly through her body, an ache she understood and suddenly feared.

'Luke. . . .' She pushed at the powerful, unyielding shoulders above her. The word came as a low moan, while his mouth teased the white skin of her throat, his tongue flicking against the frantic pulse.

'Luke. . . .' Both heard the unmistakable sound of the front door slamming.

Stephanie tore herself out of Luke's arms in panic, cold sanity reasserting itself, leaving her feeling weak and sick, while Luke stared at her with dark smoky eyes, his chest heaving.

'Oh God!' She moaned in horror, and turning on her heel, ran from the room, cannoning straight into Wayne in the hall.

He caught her and steadied her, looking down curiously at her flushed, troubled face and scantily clad body.

'Hi, you're up late,' he said lightly, and when she didn't answer, he probed, 'What's the matter?'

'Nothing—nothing at all.' Her voice sounded damningly breathless. Wayne looked past her into the dark lounge, and his eyes were suddenly narrow with amusement.

'Ah!' he said slowly, 'I see.'

Just what he saw, Stephanie dreaded to think. It couldn't be worse than the truth, a little voice in her head reminded her. She didn't even know why she was standing here. She closed her eyes and felt the hot colour pouring into her cheeks. 'You've got it all wrong,' she began anxiously.

'Of course I have, darling.' He smiled broadly and released her. 'Sweet dreams!'

'Wayne——' Guilt made her call him back, as he walked towards the lounge. She had to say something. She knew very well what he thought.

'I don't think I want to get involved,' he threw back over his shoulder, and carried on walking.

'There's nothing to get involved *in*!' Stephanie shouted in frustration.

Wayne turned then, his brows raised sceptically. 'And I thought you were a nice girl!' he reproved with an infuriating smile. He was only joking, she knew that, yet his words cut into her as though he was deadly serious.

'It's not what you think. . . .' she tried again to explain, but Wayne wasn't listening.

'Isn't there a saying about protesting too much?'

'Listen to me. . . .'

He didn't. 'I only hope Carina doesn't hear about this,' he said laughingly, and strolled into the lounge, shutting the door behind him.

Stephanie stared after him in horror. She hadn't spared Carina a thought. She covered her face with her hands, sinking on to the bottom stair. She hadn't spared Dean a thought either. All thought had been magically blanked from her mind at Luke's possessive touch. She was shaking, she felt sick. And as the final straw, she heard the voices in the lounge becoming louder. She heard Luke's voice, cold and angry, Wayne's innocent, protesting. Had Luke heard their conversation just now? She didn't stay to listen to what was going on. She shot upstairs as fast as she could, wishing with all her heart that she had never met any of them.

CHAPTER FIVE

SHE still felt depressed the next morning as she drank her breakfast coffee. Wayne found her alone in the dining room.

Stephanie sighed as she saw him. She had been hoping to get away before anyone came down. She did not feel she had the strength to face any of them this morning, so she kept her eyes lowered, waiting for him to make the first move.

She was aware of him sitting down opposite her, heard him pouring coffee.

'Morning!' His greeting was bright, hearty.

Still she did not look at him. 'Good morning,' she replied calmly.

'It looks like it's going to be a beautiful day.'

Wayne was staring at her. She looked up and their eyes met briefly, his veering away immediately.

'Yes.' She half-smiled, still too embarrassed by what had happened the night before to be able to act naturally. It was guilt, she realised sardonically, guilt at her own behaviour, at her own stupid weakness. Guilt had been her overriding emotion ever since she arrived in England. 'Yes, it does.' She looked out of the long windows pretending interest in the cloudless skies outside.

Wayne got up and filled a plate with bacon and eggs from the dishes on the long sideboard. 'Aren't you having anything to eat?' He looked at the empty plate and unused cutlery in front of her.

'I'm not hungry, thanks.' She quickly sipped her coffee, desperately trying to pull herself together.

'Listen, Stephanie.' Wayne sat down again, leaning towards her earnestly. 'I want to—well, I want to apologise for last night.'

Stephanie looked at him briefly. She felt herself flushing, felt the embarrassment crawling over her.

'Wayne, please, I——'

'No, let me finish. I'm feeling pretty lousy about it. I had a bad evening and I drank too much. I was bloody rude to you and I'm sorry.' He smiled wryly. 'If it's any consolation, Luke certainly tore me off a strip or two!'

Stephanie smiled. 'I did hear raised voices.' It wasn't so bad after all. Wayne was genuinely apologetic.

He grimaced. 'One raised voice. I hardly got the chance to open my mouth!'

'Let's forget it, shall we?' All she wanted was to push the whole incident from her mind.

'Suits me.' Wayne forked his food into his mouth as though ravenously hungry, obviously more cheerful now.

'Are you working today?' Stephanie asked casually.

'You bet!' Now the boss is back, it's noses to the grindstone for all of us.'

'Don't you mind working for your cousin?' she asked curiously. Wayne didn't seem the sort of young man to take orders very easily. In that sense, he was very like Dean.

Wayne shrugged. 'Luke's the boss—it's his empire and I'm glad to work for him. He's the sort of man you can trust with your life.'

Stephanie could believe that. She had felt it herself—inexplicable really, when he frightened her so. Wayne's implicit confidence and respect, somehow didn't surprise her either. Luke was the sort of man who commanded those qualities in all around him, commanded them effortlessly.

'You're close to him?' she asked, surprising herself with her own open interest.

Wayne regarded her speculatively for a second, then returned his attention to his plate before replying. 'Close isn't the word I'd use. I can't think of anybody who's actually close to Luke.' He smiled with a secret, almost malicious pleasure. 'Carina would surely like to be, though!'

Stephanie bit her lip. Are they lovers? she wanted to ask, but didn't.

'Oh.' She tried to sound uninterested, noncommittal.

'Luke's not an easy man to get to know, or to get close to.' Wayne hadn't been fooled for a moment by her pretended lack of interest, and continued. 'My uncle and aunt died when Luke was young. He practically brought himself up, and I guess that made him tough and self-contained. He doesn't need anybody.'

Again, Stephanie could hear the respect in his voice. She could imagine Wayne hero-worshipping his cousin when they were both younger. And she could hear perhaps a trace of envy in his voice, and that made her like him more. It made him more human.

'Lucky for him,' she remarked drily, and poured herself more coffee, feeling hungry enough to tackle a thin piece of toast now that her tension had dissolved.

Wayne laughed. 'Lucky for all of us, except Carina. Where is she, by the way?'

Stephanie explained about the phone call, not hearing the door behind her swinging open as she talked. 'Oh, and that reminds me, I want to go into the nearest town to buy a few things. Can you tell me about the buses or the trains or whatever?'

'I'll drive you.' The low, cool voice sent a shiver along her spine. She had not heard Luke come into the room, but now he sat down, indolently pouring himself a cup of coffee, his eyes unreadable, his mouth curved with amusement at her sudden confusion.

Stephanie stared blindly down at the polished table, cursing the colour that was pouring embarrassingly into her face, the remembered touch of his mouth, the searching hunger of his hands, filling her with shame and a humiliating weakness.

'I'll be driving into town in half an hour's time,' he expanded coolly. 'You're welcome to a lift.'

'There you are, problem solved,' Wayne said brightly, looking at her.

'I . . .' She was lost for words. She didn't want to be alone with Luke. She would rather have walked to the nearest town rather than accept a lift from him. The very thought of it filled her with fear and another, insidious emotion, that she did not examine too closely.

She glanced covertly at Wayne. He was still looking at her expectantly. She could also feel Luke's green eyes disturbingly fixed on her.

'I . . . I don't want to put you to any trouble . . .' she began weakly, already knowing that she had lost.

'It's no trouble,' he assured her levelly, aware that she had not once raised her eyes to his.

Stephanie swallowed nervously. What could she do? Wayne had already suspected that something was going on. She couldn't refuse Luke's offer without making a big deal of the whole situation.

'Well, if you're sure . . . thank you.' She raised resentful eyes towards him, her glance resting on the hard line of his mouth.

'Be ready in half an hour,' he said quietly, as she got to her feet, and she could hear the laughter in his voice. They both knew he had won and her resentment grew.

In her room, as she brushed and plaited her hair, she fiercely decided that under no circumstances would she let him know how she feared him. It was only a car ride, after all, nothing to panic about. She sighed. Why was she so nervous, then?

Her hard-won calmness was instantly dissolved, however, when she walked downstairs twenty minutes later to find Luke waiting for her in the high-ceilinged hall. She glanced discreetly at him as she covered the distance between them. He looked tall and disturbing in jeans and a dark green corduroy shirt open at the neck. His eyes narrowed on her as she came to him, the sunlight shimmering in her pale hair.

'Ready?' One slow expressionless glance took in her tight jeans and sleeveless cotton blouse, to bring a rush of colour to her cheeks.

'I'd really rather catch a bus,' she said stiffly.

'Why?' he taunted softly. 'Who are you afraid of, Stephanie? Me, or yourself?'

The mockery was unhidden and she glared at him angrily. 'I'm afraid of nobody!' she retorted tremulously, the lie obvious.

'Fine, let's go then.' He smiled almost gently and indicated that she should precede him out into the brilliant sunshine and towards the long silver car.

He opened the passenger door for her and she slid into the low leather seat, her eyes firmly turned away from him, burning with anger. She was making such a fool of herself, and he seemed to be taking advantage of that fact, finding it all *so* amusing!

Seconds later he slid in beside her, and she averted her face, staring out of the window at her side, as the car roared into life. The town was almost twenty miles from the house, and Stephanie gradually forgot her anger and antagonism, as she stared out over the green fields to the sea beyond—so different in the sunlight.

It was beautiful, she thought with wonder, the wild flowers at the roadside, the thick hedgerows— everything was green, a paler, richer green than at home.

Luke pressed a button on the dashboard and the wide sun roof slid open over her head. She looked up and watched the almost cloudless sky as the car shot along the narrow roads.

'It's lovely,' she said aloud, unable to keep her delight, or her need to share it, out of her voice. 'And so warm today. I thought yesterday was the best I could expect from the English summer.'

Luke cast her a sidelong glance, his eyes leaving the road for a second, and laughed. 'This weather isn't exactly usual, you know,' he admitted wryly.

'I don't care. Today is all that matters,' she told him recklessly, because the beauty of her surroundings had soothed her, and because after today, she really would have to tackle all the problems that faced her.

'You mean that?' Luke queried softly, and something in his voice made her heart slowly pound.

'Of course I do.' She glanced at the hard lines of his profile, at the strong tanned hands on the steering wheel and knew that her words were almost a commitment to him, that suddenly they weren't talking about the weather at all. She took a deep shaking breath and turned her head away, confused by the sudden tension in the expensive confines of the car.

The town was on the coast, gulls screaming overhead as they pulled into the car park. Stephanie jumped out as soon as the car slid to a halt, feeling a desperate need for fresh air. Her heart was racing and even deep breathing didn't seem to slow it. She stood staring blindly across the car park towards the main street, her thoughts in chaos, visibly jumping as

Luke's hand gently touched her shoulder. It was a light impersonal touch, but it seemed to reach something deep inside her, and she whirled to look at him, the sunlight blinding her to everything but the cool politeness in his eyes and the shining darkness of his hair.

'My business should keep me tied up for a couple of hours, but will you have lunch with me?' She was silent for a moment, wondering what to do, searching his face for signs of that violent, possessive desire she had sometimes glimpsed. 'It's only lunch,' he said teasingly, looking down into her anxious eyes.

She didn't really have much choice, she told herself, a smile tugging at the corners of her mouth, unable to resist him. Who could have resisted such charm? When he was in this calm teasing mood, she liked him very much. Too much.

As he said, it was only lunch. She had made enough of a fool of herself already.

'Yes, I'd like that,' she said at last, and smiled, thinking how churlish it would have been to refuse.

'Good.' Luke smiled back at her, and their eyes met and held, until Stephanie broke the contact and looked away.

They agreed to meet three hours later, and Stephanie wandered around the shops and along the crowded sea-front promenade, mingling with the brightly-dressed summer tourists who seemed to cram the town, and she managed to buy everything she needed for her painting of the bay, as well as a pale green velvet skirt, with a wide tight waistband and a full skirt. Green was becoming one of her favourite colours.

Mid-morning, she had coffee in a crowded tea-shop, and as she walked to the clock tower where she had arranged to meet Luke, she caught herself singing, and realised with a faint shock that she was actually happy, happier than she had been for ages, since well before this visit to England. Maybe it was because she was actually doing something today instead of mooning around the house, waiting for Carina to sort out an appointment with her father's solicitors.

She was only a few minutes late, but Luke was already waiting for her. She saw him first as she rounded the corner, watched him, waiting for him to see her, her eyes drawn to the powerful magnificence of his body and that lithe, cat-like grace, so unusual in a man of his physique.

Then she felt his eyes on her, and lowered her head, all at once intensely conscious of herself, conscious of the way she was walking and the swing of her hips and the jeans that she suddenly realised were far too tight. She reached him flushed and breathless and fiercely determined that he shouldn't see the effect he was having on her.

'Hello.' She managed a brilliant smile, looking up into his dark face.

His eyes narrowed on her upturned mouth. 'Did you get everything you wanted?'

Stephanie held up her parcels. 'Yes, everything,' she replied, marvelling at her own outward calm.

Luke took them from her, his cool fingers brushing hers, and she didn't protest, even though she was more than capable of managing them herself.

'Where would you like to eat?' he asked, as they strolled down the narrow, crowded streets.

'Somewhere small, a café perhaps,' she replied immediately. She wasn't dressed or sufficiently sure of herself for the intimacy of an expensive restaurant.

'Okay.' Luke seemed happy to leave the choice to her.

But all the cafés and small restaurants they tried

were full to bursting with lunchtime trade and tourists; some even had queues for tables.

Finally Luke turned to her. 'I don't think we're going to have much luck—it's the height of the tourist season, so we can either go to a larger restaurant——' he paused, then seeing her dismay, said, 'or we could buy some food and have a picnic.'

Stephanie smiled delightedly. 'A picnic sounds lovely!'

'A picnic it is, then.' Before she realised it, she had let her hand slide into the hand he held out, and they were walking back into the heart of the town. His fingers were cool around her own, gentle, and yet she could feel their immense strength, and it made her heart lurch violently.

Was a picnic such a good idea? she wondered, glancing covertly at his profile. She remained silent, though, and allowed Luke to buy French bread, cheese and pâté, juicy peaches and wine, then allowed her hand to stay within his, as they strolled back to his car, remembering his taunt earlier that morning.

She would be bright and cool and she wouldn't give a thing away, she decided as he held open the passenger door of the car.

'Where are we going?' she asked lightly, as he switched on the engine and the car roared into life.

'I know the perfect spot—wait and see,' he smiled, a brief hard smile that warmed the cool depths of his eyes.

She watched his brown hands on the steering wheel as he deftly manoeuvred the car out of the car park, and lapsed into silence. Somewhere inside her, beneath the vague knot of worry, she still felt happy. The sun was so bright and warm, the road in front of them hazy, buzzing with insects.

Luke too, was silent as he drove, but for once the silence between them wasn't tense, it was almost companionable. Soon they were pulling off the road, down a narrowed dirt track. Stephanie looked around and could see nothing but fields and trees.

Luke glanced at her. 'We'll have to walk from here,' he said expressionlessly, bringing the car to a halt and reaching into the back for the food.

Stephanie slid out, lifting her face to the sun, and allowed him to lead the way through the trees to a small glinting stream almost lost in the long lush grass.

'Oh!' She was dazed by the beauty of the scene before her, so different from her home, so gentle and green. 'It's beautiful!'

'Yes, beautiful.' Luke's eyes were on her, his voice faintly harsh. She did not grasp the significance in what he said, still gazing at the trees full of blossom, at the wild flowers.

Then they sat down in the long soft grass and Luke made her laugh as they ate the food he had bought, deliberately putting her at ease with him. She found herself ravenously hungry, having only nibbled at a piece of toast at breakfast. The bread tasted delicious, the cheese strong and mellow, the peaches very sweet, and she drank the wine he poured for her, licking her lips appreciatively.

'That was lovely,' she said at last with a contented sigh, as she wiped her hands. 'It's true, isn't it, what they say, about food tasting better outdoors?'

Luke smiled, 'The company has a lot to do with it.'

Stephanie looked at him uncertainly. 'I wish you wouldn't.'

'Wouldn't what?' His eyes were amused.

'I wish you wouldn't say things ... like that.' She felt foolish as she heard her own words. So much for keeping cool and not giving anything away!

'That you're good company?' There was a lazy mockery in his voice.

'You're too direct.' She didn't look at him as she made the complaint.

He shrugged, smiling. 'It's the way I am. Why does it worry you so much?'

'It doesn't. I just think. . . .' She didn't even know herself what she was trying to say.

'Mm?' he smiled, waiting.

Stephanie had the feeling he was laughing at her, and ridiculously that hurt, stinging her into saying, 'I'm engaged to somebody else—you shouldn't say . . . the things you say.'

'Ah,' he laughed, 'I see!'

'I don't think you do,' she said stiffly, wondering why she was spoiling such a lovely afternoon.

'Oh, I do, Stephanie, but if you're honest, you'll admit that you haven't spared Sangster so much as a thought this afternoon.' She saw the sudden hardness in his eyes as he spoke.

'That's not true!' she protested, depressed by the realisation that she was lying to him and to herself, and that he knew it.

'Liar.' Luke spoke so quietly that she couldn't be sure whether he actually spoke at all. Perhaps it was her own guilt, perhaps she was reading *his* thoughts for a change. The hardness in his eyes was gone, replaced by a cool taunting mockery.

'I don't want to talk about Dean. I've told you before, it's none of your business.' Stephanie averted her face, sipping the strong wine as though it was water.

Luke swore softly. 'Dammit, when are you going to open your eyes?' he demanded harshly. 'When are you going to realise that if you marry him, you're going to regret it for the rest of your life?'

'It's nothing to do with you,' she repeated stonily,

feeling the tears gathering in her eyes at his harshness, at the easy way he could bring all her doubts clamouring into her mind anew.

'Of course it damn well is!' She listened to the anger in his voice and shivered. It was always between them, Luke's anger that she was engaged to Dean. They would never be friends. She almost laughed out loud, that she had thought such a thing. Friends? She must be going mad! Luke wasn't the sort of man one had as a friend. She had seen the desire in his eyes. He did not want friendship.

'Why is it your business?' she asked stubbornly. 'Why?'

His eyes held hers, effortlessly. 'You know why. What do you want? Do you want to hear me say how I desire you? How I want you?' he queried expressionlessly, all traces of anger gone.

'No!' She felt her stomach turning over, reaction to his words shuddering inside her.

'I could tell you things that would have you running for cover like a frightened rabbit,' Luke continued sardonically, ignoring her panic, the restless movements of her hands.

'Stop it!' she cried, her face running scarlet with colour as she hurriedly got to her feet. She *wouldn't* listen to him.

Luke eyed her narrowly. 'Scared?' he asked softly.

'Just leave me alone!' Stephanie retorted, and walked down towards the stream, watching the clear fast water running over brown stones. She had provoked him, she supposed, probably because she still couldn't really believe that he wanted her. It was crazy—a man like Luke Baroda, a man with his charisma, his power and wealth. It must be some sort of game to him, she thought, very unsure of herself. Perhaps it gives him some sort of thrill to pursue those things he can't have. No, she was being unfair. She was being nasty.

She glanced quickly over her shoulder. He was still sitting on the grass, his body relaxed, graceful, and he was watching her, she could almost feel the probe of his eyes.

He was so clever, so perceptive. She felt as though she was made of glass. He knew what she thought, what she was about to think—he could read her like a book. If she'd had any sense at all, she would have refused his offer of a lift to town, she would never have allowed herself to sit in the long grass sharing food with him.

She pushed back her hair and folded her arms protectively around her body. She trusted Luke, and that was where the trouble lay. Fool, she chastised herself sternly. Fool! How *could* she trust him? She hardly knew him, and she had seen for herself that ruthless streak, the hardness that sometimes blanked his eyes.

She kicked off her sandals and sat down on the bank of the stream, allowing her bare feet to trail in the icy cold water. Oh yes, she was a fool. Luke probably thought she knew what she was doing. He probably thought that she was willing to have an affair with him, Dean being out of sight and out of mind. Perhaps her behaviour had even encouraged him, she thought confusedly.

Pretending to look along the bank, she glanced back at him out of the corner of her eye. He hadn't moved. He was leaning back against the trunk of a tree, his hands linked behind his head, drawing her attention to the powerful lines of his chest. He looked as though he was asleep, perfectly still, his body relaxed. But even when he was asleep, he was still dangerous, she thought, and smiled. Her feelings for him were so confused. Already he had great power over her emotions—and that was very worrying.

She lay back, feeling the sharp, dry grass tickling her skin through the thin cotton of her blouse. Why worry about it on such a beautiful day? she thought lazily. The sun burned behind her closed eyelids, an orange glare. She heard the insects and the running stream, felt the stillness of the scented air and felt happily tired. Luke was asleep and she had nothing to worry about.... I shouldn't have drunk so much wine, she thought drowsily, and drifted off into a light sleep....

How much later it was when she woke, she had no idea, but she jumped into wakefulness, her mind still full of the strange, frightening dreams that had haunted her sleep.

'Luke.' She opened her eyes, his name on her lips.

'Yes?' He was beside her, propped up on one elbow, staring down at her. His voice was deep.

She closed her eyes again. 'Nothing. I'm sorry.'

He hadn't been beside her when she'd fallen asleep. She lay perfectly still, feeling embarrassed and rather foolish. Had he been watching her as she slept? She couldn't bear to think that he had.

He was still and silent, yet his presence, so near, was almost tangible, stretching her nerves.

'What time is it?' she asked in a small voice, when the silence became almost too much to bear.

Luke lifted his tanned arm. 'Ten past three.'

Stephanie opened her eyes in surprise. 'Shouldn't we be getting back?' She dared to look up into the dark planes of his face, and her heart began to hammer. Those cool green eyes held hers, shadowed with an emotion she did not recognise, and all the relaxation seemed to drain from her body, leaving her brittle and tense, even her throat aching with a dry tension.

'We can leave whenever you want,' he said softly,

still staring at her. Her eyes dropped, resting on his brown throat, where a pulse beat hurriedly. She gazed at it in fascination. It was beating too fast, she thought hazily, and as the realisation sank in her skin seemed to run with fire.

'Luke. . . .' Her voice was a whisper now, she seemed unable to move a muscle, as her eyes gazed blindly into his.

Of their own volition she saw her hands lifting, her fingers tentatively touching his throat. She was hypnotised by the unsmiling darkness of his eyes, the smooth touch of his skin beneath her fingertips. And it was only when he began to lower his black head, and she realised his intentions, what she herself had invited, that she seemed to wake from the trance that held her, sharply turning away her head in panic.

'No——!' The protest was torn from her. 'I want to go back. . . .'

Luke's eyes were intent on her lips. 'You had the chance,' he said harshly, his cool breath fanning her cheek, clean and erotic.

'I want to ring Dean,' she said desperately, hoping that by mentioning him she could drive some sort of a wedge between Luke and herself.

But it only made him angry. His mouth suddenly tightened and a curious blankness shuttered his eyes. His hand moved, tangling roughly in her hair to hold her head still as his mouth touched hers. The kiss was almost brutal, bruising her lips apart with something much deeper than anger. Shock held Stephanie still for a second, then she began to fight him. Instinctively, her hands pushed at the unyielding hardness of his chest, at the powerful muscled shoulders above her. He had moved and she was pinned to the grass by the weight of his thighs and his strength was too much for her. So she lay passive, still shocked, staring up at the cloudless blue sky, as Luke's warm angry mouth trailed its fire across her face, to the softness of her throat.

He lifted his head then, staring down at her with eyes that glittered. 'Damn you, Stephanie,' he muttered harshly, and she was shocked by the raw violence in his voice, not understanding it.

Something was happening to her. She looked into his eyes, her mind not comprehending what she saw there but her body responding to it desperately. Her heart turned over, and it must have shone in her face, because Luke drew a hard uneven breath, his hands framing her face, his mouth finding hers again, this time with no violence or savagery, but with a hunger that he could not disguise.

Stephanie's response was immediate, and so fierce that she was confused and overwhelmed by the sheer force of it.

She heard him groan as her mouth moved beneath his.

'Put your arms around me,' he murmured against her lips, the words ragged and unsteady, and she lifted her hands to his shoulders, tentatively shaping the heavy muscles beneath the thin shirt, knowing the deep pleasure of touching him, of answering his need. It was there in her stomach, that hot sweet ache of desire, a need that she could not deny or control.

Luke was kissing her throat now, his tongue against the quickening pulse, his fingers deftly unbuttoning her blouse, pushing it from her shoulders, tracing the fragile bones, his mouth following, burning her skin. She moaned softly and her own fingers threaded through the thickness of his dark hair. The clean male scent of his body filled her nostrils, the scent of the grass crushed beneath her, of wild summer flowers.

His hands touched lower, her bra no barrier to his

seeking fingers. She gasped as he touched her naked breasts, the nipples stiff and hard beneath his palms. No man had ever touched her so intimately or with such knowledge or passion before in her life. Luke's desire made her tremble. She could feel the aroused heat of his body against hers, urgent, demanding response. She didn't remember opening his shirt, but suddenly it was open wide, revealing the hard lines of his chest, rough with fine dark hair that arrowed down to the flatness of his stomach.

She touched him, almost unaware of what she was doing, drowning in pleasure as his mouth teased her aching breasts, her hands tangling in his hair to hold him closer, arching her body to him in innocent abandon. Her senses were filled with him as he aroused her in a way she had never been aroused before. It was an awakening that reached some deep untouched part of her soul and changed her for ever.

She stared at his smooth tanned skin, at his strong, beautiful hands, at the hair on his body. She felt the heavy pounding of his heart against her breasts. She couldn't stop looking at him. He was holding her now, arching over her, their bodies coming close, touching in the most satisfying way. Stephanie closed her eyes, all thought lost, all sense of time spinning away from her. Her lips parted to whisper his name, and then in confused surprise she felt his body stiffen and he was moving, moving away. She felt the warm summer breeze touching her bare skin as he left her.

'Don't go. . . .' she whispered, her hands reaching for him, trying to pull him back, unaware of her own actions, knowing only the need inside herself that he had so expertly aroused.

But Luke evaded her and sat up in one lithe movement, so that she could not see his face as he gazed away across the stream to the trees beyond. She drew a deep breath, closing her eyes as the feelings faded and cold, painful reality intruded. What was she doing? *What the hell was she doing?* A wave of humiliation swept over her, scarlet colour pouring into her cheeks. Had she gone mad, letting him touch her, letting him make love to her like that?

Dean's face rose unbidden into her mind on a wave of pain, and all she wanted to do was to disappear. She wanted the ground to split open and swallow her whole.

Luke was moving, searching his pockets, finally extracting a packet of cigarettes. He glanced at her with blank eyes, offering her the packet. 'Want one?'

Stephanie shook her head, unable to say a word to him.

He turned away, and she hated him for his composure, until she watched him place a cigarette between his lips and light it, and saw that his hand was unsteady. He wasn't as calm and composed as he seemed to be. She also noticed that his shoulders were hunched, very tense, and cursed herself for watching him so intently.

That brought her to her senses and she sat up jerkily, pulling together her clothes with fingers that shook so much, it took what seemed like ages to button her blouse.

She could think of nothing but her own self-contempt and all she wanted to do was to get away from him.

She glanced at the wide line of his shoulders. 'I'll have that cigarette now, please,' she said in a shaking little voice, because she needed something to do, and smoking might calm her down a little.

In silence, Luke offered her the packet, his narrowed eyes scanning her face carefully. Her trembling fingers reached for one. He lit it for her, still watching, and she turned away immediately, dragging the smoke deep into her lungs, thankful that he had not spoken. She did not want to speak to him, and she wished desperately that she did not have to rely on him for a lift back to the house—his house.

She wanted to think everything out logically, everything that had happened that afternoon, but her thoughts were chaotic. She felt as though she was verging on hysteria, any slip might push her over the edge. So she let her mind drift uneasily and smoked her cigarette, wondering when they would leave.

But as the minutes passed and Luke did not move, the heavy silence between them began to get to her, and in the end she said, 'Shouldn't ... shouldn't we be driving back?' Her voice sounded high and stupidly unnatural.

Luke turned and looked at her, and she could read no expression in the bleak depths of his eyes.

'Yes. Stephanie. . . .'

'Good,' she cut in desperately, knowing he was about to say something important, and not feeling strong enough to take it. She stood up, brushing the grass from her jeans. 'I'll collect everything.'

She turned away from him, but she had only taken a few steps when he caught her arm, pulling her round, forcing her to face him. He had moved so fast and so silently that she was shocked for a moment to find him beside her. His shirt still hung open, the tanned, hair-roughened expanse of his chest drawing her compulsive gaze, angering her, because he still had the power to make her feel weak.

'Don't touch me!' she spat at him, trying to push away his hand without success.

'Stephanie, for God's sake listen to me!' His eyes scorched her, his hands bruising her bones.

'I don't want to!' She struggled in his grasp. She

couldn't bear his touch just at that moment, and she certainly couldn't bear to talk about what had just happened between them.

'Well, you're going to have to,' he told her immovably.

'Why?' She was stubborn, and his mouth tightened with impatience.

'Do you want to leave it like this?'

Stephanie glared at him with brilliant, fevered eyes. 'I don't care, but I don't want an apology.' Perversely, she thought she would burst into tears if he apologised.

'You'll hear it anyway,' he told her grimly, 'because I *am* sorry—it shouldn't have happened that way. I was angry and I shouldn't have touched you. It was never my intention to....' He stopped abruptly, biting back the words, and his grip on her shoulders loosened slightly as though he realised he was hurting her. There was silence for a few seconds, then he said quietly, 'I have no excuse to offer you, but I am sorry.'

Stephanie bit her lip. It was the final humiliation. He actually regretted kissing her, touching her!

'And that makes it all fine, does it?' she said in a cold, trembling voice.

'You know damn well it doesn't!'

She was deliberately making him angry, she knew that, but she didn't care. 'Your apology is a waste of time, then, isn't it?'

'It's necessary,' he corrected her tautly.

She felt the tears pricking the back of her eyelids, felt the aching tension in the back of her throat. He was angry, but he was totally in control, she thought bitterly. She wanted to shake him out of that impassive calmness.

What had happened meant nothing to him, he already regretted it. She was not yet sure what had happened to her when he touched her so possessively, so intimately, but something had—something deep and confusing and worrying. Something she felt sure would change her life when she recognised it.

'Will you be apologising to Dean as well?' she asked flatly.

Luke's eyes narrowed. 'Will you?' he countered softly.

'You forced me. . . .' She didn't get the chance to say another word.

'Crying rape, Stephanie?' Cold violence threaded his voice and an icy mockery hardened his eyes. She had succeeded in making him very angry indeed. 'Don't kid yourself, sweetheart. You wanted me— almost as much as I wanted you. I could have had you and you wouldn't have raised a finger to stop me,' he told her with brutal deliberation.

'You're a cold uncaring bastard!' she exclaimed hysterically, shocked by the raw truth of his words. 'I hate you!'

She was insulting him because he spoke the truth, they both knew that. The knowledge hung between them in the summer air, making a mockery of her harsh words.

'Of course you do.' His voice was almost gentle, and he half smiled, taking her chin between his hard fingers and forcing her to look at him. 'It isn't over, though, Stephanie, you know that.'

She didn't answer him.

'All you have to do is wake up,' he told her expressionlessly, then he released her, turning away abruptly.

'Luke——' she began.

'It's time we were moving,' he said, and walked towards the car, leaving her still and shaking and desperately confused.

CHAPTER SIX

As soon as they reached the house Stephanie ran inside, glad to be out of the car and the heavy silent atmosphere they had both endured on the way back. Not a word had been spoken, and the tension was suffocating. She had glanced at Luke once. His profile had been as hard as granite, the only evidence that it wasn't a mask of stone being the muscle flicking along his jaw.

She had heaved a sigh of pure relief as the car pulled up in front of the house, and although she knew it was ungracious, she didn't thank him for the picnic, but merely bolted from the car and ran straight upstairs to her room.

Once inside, she pulled off all her clothes and took a cool shower, the invigorating jets of water cleaning her hot body and strangely, clearing her mind.

She had overracted, she thought ruefully, as she sat by the open window fifteen minutes later, slowly smoking a cigarette. And if she was honest with herself—and it was about time she was—her furious anger with Luke had stemmed from her own frustration. She had wanted him—oh, how she had wanted him! Wanted him so badly that his rejection had squashed her, leaving her eager for some sort of childish revenge. What she had been hoping for, she did not know. What she did know for sure was that no man had ever made her feel the way Luke had. For the first time in her life she had felt that craving, that awakening need. . . .

Her mind halted, refusing to carry her thoughts on

99

to their logical conclusion. She stubbed out the cigarette and got to her feet, pacing restlessly around the luxurious room. No, she thought, no. But the deliberate blanking of her mind was only putting off something that had to be confronted. It had to be faced. And she found that she was shaking as she finally admitted that Dean had never been able to arouse in her the feelings that Luke could arouse, merely by his touch.

Allowing Luke to make love to her had been wrong, very wrong—and yet if he had not drawn back, she would have let him take her. That was the truth, and it made her shudder with fear.

She had been totally unaware of everything except Luke's mouth, Luke's hands and Luke's body. The moment he kissed her she should have stopped him, had wanted to stop him, until that terrifyingly sweet weakness had gripped her, wiping every objection away.

When Dean kissed her, she found it pleasurable, reassuring, but nothing compared to the earth-shattering touch of Luke's mouth. Could she possibly marry Dean knowing that? Wouldn't it be unfair to him? More unfair to him than to her?

She sank into a chair, deathly pale. Of course it would be unfair, and she couldn't do it, she couldn't hurt him that way.

There was only one course of action open to her: she had to break off the engagement. She touched the sapphire ring on her wedding finger and found that she was crying, the blue stone shattering into a million tiny pieces through her tears. She would have to tell Dean that she couldn't marry him. It would be the hardest thing she had ever done.

I love him, she thought fiercely, but even the thought was hollow. She couldn't have responded to

Luke the way she had done, if she had loved Dean.

Luke had been right all along, damn him. She loved Dean as a brother, as a dear close friend. Her life on Moahu, so beautifully easy, had blinded her, left her a child in a woman's body. She had always had Dean to lean on. She had let things drift because she had not known any better.

It could have been anybody, any man, but it had been Luke who had ripped the veils from her eyes and forced her to face up to the reality of life as a grown woman. She put her head in her hands, and began to sob like a baby. She didn't feel like going down to dinner, she certainly didn't feel like facing Luke. It would be in his eyes, his remembrance, his knowledge of her, mocking her, taunting her.

Tattered pride finally came to her rescue. She would not allow him to see how right he had been. She would face him as though nothing had happened, as though she had already forgotten his lovemaking.

She carelessly pulled a brush through her hair, frowning at her reflection in the dressing table mirror. And, of course, there was Carina and Wayne. She couldn't let them see anything was wrong.

She threw down the brush, feeling utterly miserable, and pulled from the wardrobe the first dress that came to hand. It was silk, violet and blue in delicate patterns. It suited her perfectly, although the knowledge brought her no pleasure tonight. She was just sliding a gold bangle on to her wrist when Carina knocked on the door.

Stephanie sighed with relief when she saw her half-sister. She had been terrified that it might be Luke.

'You're back,' she said, managing a stiff little smile.

'As you can see.' Carina strolled into the room, dressed for dinner, stunningly beautiful in black, adorned with discreetly shining platinum jewellery.

'I'd like a word, if you have a moment.' She did not smile, and her eyes flicked coolly over Stephanie, assessing her.

'Of course—sit down.' Stephanie indicated a chair, a feeling of apprehension tightening her stomach. Carina seemed in a particularly bad mood tonight. 'Successful trip?' she asked brightly.

Carina shrugged, lifting a cigarette from the gold case in her hand, lighting it with delicate grace.

'The solicitors will be here next Tuesday at noon,' she told Stephanie briefly.

It was just under a week away, too long to be under the same roof as Luke Baroda, but what choice did she have?

'Oh—good. I'll be glad when it's all sorted out.'

Carina looked at her sharply. 'Will you?' There was a wealth of meaning in her cool voice.

'Yes, of course—won't you?'

'That's not really what I was getting at, as I'm sure you know.' Carina exhaled smoke in a long stream, her red nails at her throat.

Stephanie frowned, genuinely puzzled. 'I don't know what you mean, I for one really will be glad when it's all over. I want to get home, and I'm sure you won't be sorry to see me go.' There was no point in being subtle with Carina and Stephanie felt too depressed tonight to fence with her.

Her half-sister smiled at that. 'Are you sure you want to get home?' Her pale eyes held Stephanie's, faintly hostile.

Stephanie gave an exasperated sigh. 'Carina, if you've got something to say to me, I'd appreciate it if you came to the point.'

'I believe you spent the day with Luke,' the other woman suddenly shot out, getting to the point immediately.

'Yes, he gave me a lift into town, there were some things I wanted to buy, then we went for a picnic.' Stephanie tried to keep her voice cool, but the remembrance of Luke's lovemaking brought a rush of colour to her face that she knew Carina's sharp eyes did not miss.

'How very clever of you, arranging all that,' said Carina, her voice slightly acid and Stephanie suddenly realised what she was getting at.

'It wasn't like that,' she protested quickly, but could not meet her half-sister's eyes. It hadn't been planned by her, she desperately wished it hadn't happened. How could she convince Carina of that? How could she even convince herself?

'Honestly, Carina——'

'I really don't know,' the other woman cut in, her voice distinctly bored. 'However, I do want to give you a word of advice.' She paused, stubbing out her cigarette, and Stephanie bowed her head, fully aware of what was coming.

'Men like Luke are very rare,' Carina continued delicately. 'Women know that as soon as they see him. God knows, I've seen them throwing themselves at him, and frankly I can't blame them. I don't even blame you, although I would have thought—bearing in mind the fact that you *are* engaged to another man—that you would have displayed a little more restraint.'

'Carina, please——' Stephanie cut in, feeling very small and very guilty, her face scarlet.

But Carina merely lifted her pale hand and said flatly, 'Please allow me to finish.' She paused as though considering what to say next, then half-smiled. 'To put it crudely, I'm asking you—well, actually, telling you, to stay away from him. I've worked long and hard to get myself in this position.' She saw Stephanie's blank look and explained. 'Living under

Luke's roof—and I don't intend it all to have been for nothing. Do you understand?'

'Yes, I understand,' Stephanie said quietly, an innocent dignity stiffening her spine. 'And you can rest assured that I'm not the least interested in Luke Baroda—you're welcome to him!' she finished emphatically.

Carina was silent for a moment, scanning Stephanie's angry face as though doubting she told the truth, then she said, 'I'm glad you feel that way.'

'I do,' Stephanie reinforced firmly, thinking how unsure her half-sister must be. And with good reason, a tiny voice in her head reminded her.

But Carina was smiling, obviously relieved. 'I hope you don't mind me being so blunt. I merely thought——'

'I understand,' Stephanie cut in, biting her lip; she found the whole confrontation distinctly embarrassing. Then, even though she wanted Carina to go, she suddenly surprised herself by saying, 'You must be very close.'

Carina smiled, her eyes full of secrets—secrets, Stephanie realised with horror, that she was jealous of.

'We'll be announcing our engagement within the next few weeks—that's strictly confidential information, by the way.'

It was a bombshell, the last thing that Stephanie had expected. She thought of the way Luke had held her only hours before, and felt sick.

'Congratulations,' she heard herself saying through numb lips.

'Thank you.' Carina looked very pleased with herself, suddenly in a mood to talk, although Stephanie could not help suspecting her half-sister's motives.

'Do you know, I could hardly believe it when I

found out that father had landed a job with the Baroda Corporation. The moment I saw Luke, I knew—all that raw power, all that wealth. And God knows, I had to work like the devil to arrange dinners, chance meetings and that sort of thing. Believe me, Father's illness was a godsend!'

'Carina!' Stephanie's face was white with shock, but Carina only smiled, a hard light in her pale eyes.

'Come now, you're not that naïve, darling, you can drop the outraged innocence. Father never gave a damn about me, and I used him to get a foothold here—it was a fair deal.'

'You shouldn't talk about him like that!' Stephanie protested. It seemed that she was *that* naïve, because Carina's words, utterly believable when you looked into her eyes, did shock her—more than she would have thought possible.

'Why not?' Carina shrugged. 'He's dead, and when he was alive I never came first, not even after my mother died. Not that I really minded—it meant that I could use him without any scruples at all.'

Stephanie stared at her, open-mouthed, but beneath the shock at her half-sister's confessions she felt a pang of sympathy. In a way, Carina had been rejected by her father. It must have hurt, it must have hardened her.

'I don't believe you,' she said quietly.

'No? You'd better believe that I want Luke, and I don't intend to let *anything* get in my way.'

'Do you love him?' Stephanie was forced to ask, and Carina laughed, high icy laughter that tinkled on the air like broken glass, laughter that held no real amusement.

'I don't believe that there's any such thing as love. I want Luke for his power and for his money and because he's fantastic in bed. He knows that—I'd

never be able to fool him. We have . . .' she paused
delicately, 'an understanding, you might say.'

They were lovers, Stephanie realised. Carina was
spelling that out. Something inside her twisted
violently. Did Luke believe in love?

She looked at her half-sister, admiring her perfect
beauty, as she always did, and thought, I don't like her
very much. Carina was hard, as ruthless as Luke in
her own way. Stephanie thought of Connie. She was
hard too, but she was kind. She had a heart, and that
was where Carina lost out. Carina had no heart at all.
Life and experience had moulded her that way.

'You think I'm a cold-hearted bitch, don't you?'
Carina drawled with amusement, reading her thoughts,
and lighting another cigarette as she spoke.

'No.' It was the only thing Stephanie could say.

Carina ignored her lie. 'Well, maybe I am. I suspect
I was brought up to be, but I really don't care. You,
my dear Stephanie, on the other hand, are as soft as
butter. You'd better hurry up and marry your clever
young fiancé and let him protect you from the big bad
world out there.' Her voice was slightly scathing as she
rose to her feet, smoothing down her black skirt in
once graceful movement.

If they had been anything other than total strangers,
Stephanie would have told Carina then of her decision
not to marry Dean. Loneliness swept over her as she
watched her half-sister moving towards the door. She
had still been hoping that she and Carina would be
friends; after all, there were no other members of their
family still living.

But Carina wasn't interested, and in a way
Stephanie could understand that. It had been
Stephanie's mother who had driven the wedge
between Carina and her father, however uninten-
tionally. Carina's bitterness was ingrained from

childhood—no amount of talk would ever change it. A weak father and a stepmother who never tried to replace Carina's natural mother. There was a lot of good in Carina; she had been a child damaged by the adult world.

There was something Stephanie had to know, though, and now was as good a time as any to ask—it seemed a day for finding things out.

'Carina——' she halted her half-sister as she was leaving the room, 'there's something I'd like to ask you,' she said tentatively.

Carina turned. 'Fire away, darling.'

Stephanie didn't really know where to start. 'All those years, I wrote to Father, I ... I ... never received any reply. . . .' She wasn't even sure what she was asking, and her voice trailed off, almost in embarrassment.

'He got the letters,' Carina told her coolly, 'and he read every one of them. He really was very fond of you, you know, but, especially towards the end of his life, he was a very bitter man. The divorce changed him—he never wanted it. And there's really nothing more I can say. I suppose you reminded him of your mother, perhaps that's why he never answered your letters, but he was fond of you.'

'Thank you.' Stephanie felt her eyes filling with tears, because it didn't matter whether or not Carina was lying, Stephanie believed her kindness.

'Any time.' With a faint, almost impersonal smile Carina left the room, and Stephanie sank down into one of the chairs. What a day! she thought ruefully. She felt absolutely exhausted and she still had dinner to face. She thought about her father and about what Carina had said. Carina was going to marry Luke. Luke—Stephanie's thoughts were unwillingly drawn to him. It was difficult to believe that he was the kind of man who would try to seduce one woman when practically engaged to another. In fact, she would have sworn that he wasn't that kind of man.

She sighed heavily. But then what did she really know about him? She knew of his power, of his wealth, they were indisputable. And she also knew of his innate charm and the quality of gentleness that threaded his personality and had the power to turn her legs to water. He was an enigma, and from now on he was strictly out of bounds. She would keep out of his way for Carina's sake—and for her own.

Dinner was awkward. On the surface, it looked fine. Carina was utterly charming, her beauty lighting the room, and Wayne was talkative and amusing. But it was Luke who dominated, by the sheer force of his personality. He looked virile and powerful in a maroon velvet dinner jacket. His face was expressionless, his eyes when they rested on Stephanie's bent head were shadowed and brooding. She was deeply aware of him, only feet away, opposite her. And she was aware of every tiny movement he made, but she kept her head lowered, eating the food she felt would surely choke her, speaking only when spoken to, as Rose bustled around them all.

Once she looked up, smiling at something Wayne had said, and her eyes met Luke's. His narrowed, and their glances locked, communication like electricity passing between them. Stephanie couldn't breathe and she couldn't look away from him. She stared into the lean dark beauty of his face as though hypnotised, her skin heating—a purely subconscious reaction to what her heart and mind read in his eyes.

How long it lasted she couldn't have said, probably only a few seconds, but by the time she had the strength to drag her eyes away, she was sure that Carina and Wayne must have noticed. But when she glanced at them she realised that, amazingly, they hadn't. She didn't dare to look at Luke again but listened to his voice as he talked. It was low and attractive and it sent shivers down her spine. He was charming, witty, so brilliant, and she could feel herself falling under the spell of his magnetism, and in panic at that realisation, she escaped as soon as the meal was over.

He was predatory and dangerous, she reminded herself, as she ran up the wide staircase to her room. He was filling her thoughts too much. He belonged to Carina. That was a crazy thought. Luke Baroda belonged to nobody but himself; she had better remember that.

As she slid between the silken sheets, she counted the days to the solicitor's visit. She had to get out of this house as soon as she could. It was madness to stay.

Dean arrived late the next day. Stephanie was not at the house, she was down in the private cove, painting. It was another hot, flawless day and she was forcing herself to concentrate on what she was doing to stop herself thinking about Luke and about Carina. The painting wasn't bad, she thought, eyeing it critically, as she pushed back her blonde hair, but on the other hand, it was obvious that her heart just wasn't in it.

She glanced at her watch. Four-thirty, and she felt very thirsty. She would go back and make some coffee. It was useless to try and carry on in her present mood.

She stood up, stretching her arms over her head, the sleeveless tee-shirt she was wearing rising, exposing her skin to the sunlight, as she arched her aching back. Then storing everything away, and shoving the small canvas under her arm, she climbed the narrow cliff path back to the house.

She felt tired, hot and sticky by the time she reached

the front door. Not sleeping well the night before hadn't helped either. She heard voices from the lounge as she passed, and suddenly recognising Dean's easy laughter, she hurried in.

'Dean!'

He was sitting with Carina, a tray of coffee in front of them. They were both smiling, and he rose as she entered.

'When did you get here? I didn't know you were arriving today, or I would have been here to meet you!' Stephanie cried, hugging him.

Dean bent and briefly kissed her lips. 'That's okay, Carina has been looking after me.'

'It's been my pleasure,' Carina cut in, her voice cool and husky. Somehow her words made Stephanie feel uncomfortable. She looked at Carina's elegant sundress, at her shining hair and carefully stunning make-up, then down at her own salt-stained jeans and windblown hair. The comparison wasn't good, and she could see the same thought reflected in Dean's blue eyes.

'You didn't tell me that your fiancé is such—an attractive man,' Carina continued smoothly. She was flirting with him, Stephanie realised, as Dean's hands dropped from her shoulders, flirting with him openly.

'You didn't ask,' she replied with a very sweet smile. 'Is there any coffee left? I'm parched!'

'I'll tell Rose to make some fresh.' Carina rose gracefully to her feet. 'I'm sure you two want to be alone.' Her eyes were amused, almost patronising, and Stephanie felt herself flushing, more with irritation than anything else.

'Thank you,' she said, her slight sarcasm totally lost on Carina, who was smiling at Dean, her beauty stunning him. What on earth was she playing at? Stephanie wondered.

Then, to her relief, she was gone, Dean's admiring eyes following her every inch of the way.

Stephanie felt depression washing over her. She should have been jealous about Carina's blatant behaviour, instead she only felt irritated, and that only seemed to prove the fact that she did not love Dean the way she should. It also reminded her that Dean hadn't flown heaven knows how many thousand miles just to see her. He was after Luke.

'That's some woman,' he said under his breath as the door closed quietly.

Stephanie smiled. 'Yes, she is lovely.' Dean was like a child, pressing his nose against a toyshop window. Her words seemed to bring her to his notice for the first time.

'How's it going?' He came towards her, pulling her into his arms and kissing her fiercely. She felt the demanding touch of his lips almost clinically. It was pleasurable, but it moved nothing inside her. And although she hated herself for doing it, she found herself comparing his kiss to Luke's, and realising, pulled away from him.

'The solicitors will be here on Tuesday,' she said lightly, ignoring his frowning glance. 'After that, with any luck we'll be able to go home.'

'And Baroda?' Dean fired the question at her as though it was the only thing he was interested in.

'What about him?' She tried to keep her voice level and unconcerned.

'Come on, Stephanie!' He was impatient.

'There's nothing to say. He's here—he lives here, and as instructed, I've been *nice* to him,' she retorted bitterly, stung by his impatience, and feeling guilty, very guilty and very deceitful and very angry at the whole situation.

Dean laughed at the defiance straightening her gentle mouth. 'That's my girl!'

'Dean——'

Before she could speak, Carina reappeared with a tray of fresh coffee, pushing open the door, her eyes moving coolly from Stephanie to Dean. Perhaps she'd overheard what they'd been saying, Stephanie thought and almost laughed. Since she had arrived here, she had never seen Carina performing such menial tasks as fetching coffee. She was definitely up to something.

Dean was hurrying forward, taking the tray, very gallant, and Stephanie sighed.

'Well, I'll leave you in Carina's *capable* hands, while I go up and get changed,' she said lightly, wanting to get away.

'Fine. See you later, honey.' Dean flashed her a warm, charming smile and she had to stop herself from stamping her foot with exasperation.

Fighting not to slam the door as she left the room, Stephanie heard Carina's tinkling laughter, Dean's low amused words. They were probably laughing at her, she thought furiously, and she probably deserved it. She had been behaving abominably.

She ran upstairs, ridiculous, inexplicable tears shimmering in her eyes, not looking were she was going, so that she cannoned straight into Luke's hard body as she reached the high landing. His hands shot out, steadying her, preventing her from falling backwards down the stairs.

'Let me go,' she whispered shakily, trying to push his hands away, not raising her head.

'What's the matter?' he asked quietly.

'Nothing,' she replied stubbornly.

Still holding her, he tilted up her chin with his thumb, staring down into her tear-filled eyes. 'Nothing?' His eyes were gentle.

'Nothing,' she repeated defiantly, but her voice broke, her tears falling quickly now.

Luke flicked them away with his fingers, his mouth tight. 'You should let somebody in close to you,' he said softly. 'You can't bottle it all up for ever—you don't need to be so alone.'

Stephanie sniffed loudly. 'Are you suggesting yourself as a candidate?' she demanded huskily. 'I've been quite close enough to you, thanks!'

His laughter was deep and attractive. 'I disagree.'

That made the corners of her mouth turn up. 'Dean is downstairs with Carina, and I've just made a complete fool of myself,' she told him miserably.

'Poor Stephanie!' There was a gentle mockery in his green eyes. He was putting it all into perspective for her, and she smiled gratefully.

'Yes, poor me. Oh, I don't know why I'm acting like this.'

'You're growing up, my love,' Luke told her with a smile.

'You're so patient,' she marvelled, staring at him.

'I'm prepared to wait.' There was a deep significance in his voice that she ignored.

'Carina's so beautiful,' she said, without envy.

'Yes.' His agreement was expressionless.

'I want to be beautiful,' she said childishly, knowing that he wouldn't give a damn if she told him how Carina was flirting unashamedly with Dean.

Luke's eyes held hers. 'If you want to hear me say it, I will. You are beautiful, Stephanie—very beautiful.' There was a roughness in his voice that caught her breath in her throat.

'I . . . I didn't mean——'

'Oh yes, you did.'

He slowly bent his dark head and brushed her mouth with his. She had expected cynicism, but his lips were hungry, demanding, and despite all her efforts not to, her body swayed weakly against the hard strength of his. His hands immediately tightened on her shoulders, holding her almost roughly away from him. And then, as she looked confusedly into his narrowed eyes, she saw the cynicism she had feared.

'No games, Stephanie,' he warned her harshly.

'I don't understand . . .' Something inside her was flinching from that mocking cynicism. It hurt very badly.

Luke's face was a hard, unreadable mask, his eyes searching hers for long seconds as though he was trying to make up his mind about something.

'No,' he conceded wryly, quietly, 'I don't believe you do.' And releasing her, he walked away without a backward glance.

CHAPTER SEVEN

THE days passed quickly and the solicitor's appointment loomed nearer and nearer. And as it did, the strange feeling of foreboding nagging away in Stephanie's brain grew bigger and deeper.

She could find no real reason for it at all, and that worried her even more. There was an atmosphere in the house that she could not define, because superficially everything seemed fine, nobody was admitting anything.

The day after Dean arrived, Luke went away on business. Stephanie suspected that he had gone deliberately, but Wayne assured her that he really was needed to sort out a crisis in one of his hotels on Martinique.

Dean was irritated by Luke's disappearance. It was not how he had planned it when he had taken precious time away from the casino.

'Why the hell didn't you tell me he wouldn't be here?' he had demanded of Stephanie, as they walked together along the wave-lashed beach, the afternoon Luke left.

'I didn't know!' she protested, hurt that he actually blamed *her* for Luke's business meeting abroad.

'Well, that's great, isn't it?' he had replied sourly.

She had turned away then, hurt and vulnerable, and had heard his sigh of compunction as he caught her shoulder and pulled her against him.

'It's *not* my fault,' she had said painfully, staring up at him with bruised eyes.

'No, it isn't,' Dean had conceded with an easy smile. 'But you know how much this means to me, honey.'

'I thought you'd come here to be with me,' she had said dully.

'And so I have, but we can't mess up an opportunity like this.'

She knew he was lying. He had come because it was Luke's house and because he had expected Luke to be here.

The day had deteriorated for her after that. Now she was sitting alone in her room, staring out of the windows at the rain and the dark racing clouds.

The weather had broken, strangely symbolic, and though Stephanie hated herself for it, she missed Luke almost desperately. Had she really come to rely on his presence so much? It was a depressing thought. He was, after all, going to marry Carina, and she sighed and tried, not so successfully, to push all thoughts of him out of her mind.

The afternoon was passing with screaming slowness. She was restless and worried, and as yet she had not plucked up the courage to tell Dean that she could not marry him. It preyed on her mind every moment she spent with him. She was being so weak and so cowardly, and in consequence she was different whenever they were together. Dean, however, seemed totally unaware of the change in her. How could he not have noticed? she wondered dully, and the answer she came up with made her feel even more miserable.

Perhaps he did not care enough to notice. Stephanie had no idea how he saw her now. She had no idea how she could have lived with her own illusion of him for so many years. She had imagined him tuned to her every mood—perhaps that had been ridiculously naïve.

Seeing him with newly-matured eyes, she recognised his self-obsession. He was charming, generous and impulsive and she still loved him, even though she

now saw him as he really was, even though she knew
that love to be the wrong kind for marriage. He had
radical ideas about marriage. To him, Stephanie
wasn't a person, she was a woman, to be cherished, to
bear his children, to marry, but not to include in the
fabric of his life. He talked to her as he talked to all
women, never seriously. And she needed more. She
needed a man who listened to her, who respected her
as a person in her own right, who recognised and
responded to her intelligence, as well as desiring her
physically. It was more than Dean could ever give her,
and it made her very sad.

They had spent their days together since Luke left
for Martinique driving round the English countryside,
visiting London, acting like tourists. It had been great
fun, but marred for Stephanie by the knowledge she
was carrying around inside herself. All the time it was
just beneath the surface, as she searched for the
courage and the strength to bring it out into the open,
to tell Dean that she could not marry him.

And every day she failed to find that courage,
pretending that everything was all right, hating herself
for it, hating herself for not feeling a thing when he
kissed her so urgently. She closed her eyes wearily,
wishing, just for a second that she had not grown up,
that Luke had not taught her about desire. Would she
have married Dean and lived happily ever after?
Somehow she doubted it.

She *must* tell him today. She would go and find him
now. It was stupid and cruelly pointless to delay any
longer. For his sake, as well as her own, it had to be
now.

She got to her feet, pushing back her hair. She had
left Dean downstairs after lunch with the excuse that
she was going to rest for an hour or two. She
swallowed nervously as she left her room, walking

quickly downstairs and pushing open the lounge door before her nerve broke.

The room was empty except for Wayne, talking on the telephone. He looked up at her, smiling, and she lifted her hand, shaking her head to indicate that she did not want to interrupt, before silently withdrawing.

She wandered through the other downstairs rooms, finding them all empty, and with a puzzled frown, she returned to the lounge, to find Wayne replacing the receiver as she walked in.

'Hi,' he said brightly. 'I'm having a drink. Want one?' He strolled over to the cabinet where the drinks were kept, pouring himelf a large measure of gin.

'Have you seen Dean?' Stephanie asked casually, staring past him out of the windows, where dark clouds raced low over the whistling trees.

Wayne looked away, avoiding her eyes, she realised. 'He drove Carina up to town after lunch,' he revealed lightly. 'I don't think they're back yet.'

'London?'

Wayne nodded, and she digested the news with dismay. Somehow she had known that Dean was with Carina. Wayne was watching her now, and she consciously pulled herself together. 'Oh, I see. Well, in that case, I will have a drink. Sherry please.'

She had to act normally. She felt too vulnerable to open any of her feelings to Wayne.

'Sure.' He sounded glad to have something to do as he turned back to the cabinet. 'That was Luke on the phone,' he said, as he handed her a glass, and they both sat down.

'Really?' Stephanie could feel her heart beating uncomfortably, a hot colour staining her cheeks.

'He'll be back tomorrow for the solicitor's meeting. He asked about you,' Wayne told her with a searching glance.

'About me?' she echoed inanely, lowering her eyes.

'Yes, about you,' Wayne smiled slyly. 'You interest him a lot from what I can gather.'

Stephanie's face burned. 'Don't be silly!'

'Is it silly? I wonder. . . .'

'Wayne please——' She knew he was only teasing her, but she felt utterly embarrassed, her stomach churning at the very thought of Luke asking about her.

'I told him that you were fine, dashing around the countryside with your fiancé, having the time of your life,' Wayne continued with satisfaction, ignoring her plea.

Stephanie glared at him. 'You enjoy playing games with people, don't you?'

He laughed. 'Of course I do,' he admitted with honest charm. 'Don't you?'

'It's not something I indulge in,' she told him, disarmed by his smiling frankness.

'You ought to, you're far too serious.' He slanted her a teasing sidelong glance.

'I've got a lot on my mind——'

'Luke?' He hazarded too perceptively.

'No, not Luke,' Stephanie replied quickly, but her darkening eyes and nervous hands gave her away. 'Why on earth should I be thinking of Luke?'

'You're no good at lying either,' he said unrepentantly, his gaze narrowing over the glass he held to his lips. 'There's definitely something going on between you two—I haven't figured it out yet, but I will.'

'You seem to forget that I'm engaged to Dean,' she reminded him stiffly, amazed at how meaningless the words sounded.

'Are you telling me,' he mocked in reply, 'or reminding yourself?'

She couldn't get annoyed with him, however much she wanted to.

'You've got it all wrong,' she told him with an expensively calm smile.

'Tell me how it is, then.'

'It's not really any of your business, is it?' she retorted sweetly.

'No,' Wayne conceded, unabashed. 'But it makes life around here a lot more interesting.' He got lazily to his feet. 'Another drink?'

Stephanie hesitated. Dean was out with Carina and Luke was away. She had nothing better to do, her only alternatives the cold rainy weather, or her room. 'Yes, thank you.'

'I really don't blame you, you know. I've seen the effect Luke has on women.' Wayne handed her a refilled glass and sat down again.

'A womaniser?' Stephanie queried with grudging interest.

He shrugged. 'He was pretty wild when he was younger, and of course, we all read the newspaper stories, but—no, I wouldn't call him a womaniser. He certainly doesn't abuse the power he seems to have over members of the fair sex.' There was a slight edge of envy in Wayne's voice, and Stephanie smiled, curious to know more.

'I suppose wealth and power are always attractive,' she said casually.

'I guess so. Luke has worked long and hard for his empire, though. Nobody handed it to him on a plate.'

'Tell me,' Stephanie prompted, unable to conceal her interest any longer. Wayne smiled, his eyes glinting with mischief.

'Well, he travelled round the world after he finished university. He was away for years, nobody heard a word from him, and when he finally got back to England, we learned that he owned a hotel in the

Caribbean—he'd actually won it in a poker game, would you believe it? He'd changed too, he was harder, more cynical—I guess that's what world travel does for you. And from then on, he started working, building up his empire, and that's about it.'

He swallowed back his drink, and Stephanie digested the information with wonder. For some reason, it didn't surprise her that Luke had won his first hotel in a poker game. His recklessness frightened her, yet at the same time excited her. Dean's recklessness at the gaming tables only ever made her feel anxious and sick. Another comparison, something she found herself doing all the time now. Luke always won, and she hated herself for it.

'I hear that Luke will be getting married soon,' she remarked, because saying the words brought the truth of them home.

'That's news to me.' Wayne sat up eagerly. 'Who's the lucky girl?'

Stephanie frowned at him. He was joking. 'Carina said. . . .' She began uncomfortably, remembering with sudden horror that it had been a confidence, a confidence that she shouldn't be breaking. But she didn't get the chance to finish the sentence.

Wayne laughed incredulously. 'Luke and Carina? You're joking!'

Stephanie shook her head. 'No, I thought you were. I got the impression from Carina that . . . that it was all arranged.' Her heart twisted as she spoke the words. She could picture Carina in Luke's arms, and it hurt like mad.

'You must have got it wrong,' said Wayne, still genuinely amused, still shaking with laughter.

Stephanie doubted it. Perhaps nobody had bothered to tell Wayne. She still believed Carina, even though he seemed so adamant.

'Sounds like wishful thinking to me,' he said with a wide grin.

Stephanie shrugged and said, 'Carina sounded very sure.'

'Have you asked Luke?'

Her face burned. 'Of course not,' she said hurriedly. 'It's nothing to do with me.'

Wayne's silence and the knowing look he cast her was infuriating. Both heard the slam of the front door and Carina's bright laughter. Stephanie felt her body stiffening as the couple entered the room. Dean looked guilty, she saw with surprise, his eyes veering away from hers.

'Where have you two been until this late hour?' Wayne asked lazily.

'You know very well. I had some shopping to do,' Carina informed him sweetly, dumping a dozen bags bearing the names of exclusive London shops on one of the sofas. 'Dean very kindly drove me up to town. I hope you don't mind me borrowing your fiancé for the afternoon, Stephanie.' Without saying so, she managed to give the impression of friendly intimacy between herself and Stephanie's fiancé.

'Very cosy,' Wayne remarked, watching her.

Carina smiled like a satisfied cat. 'If you've got nothing better to do, darling, you can fix Dean and me a drink.' She sat down, elegantly kicking off her high-heeled shoes. 'I'm exhausted!'

Stephanie watched Wayne following instructions and mixing drinks for Carina and Dean.

'I had some business to attend to,' Dean told her, sitting down next to her.

He was explaining himself, she realised with dismay. She smiled at him, not knowing what to say, wishing that he hadn't said anything at all.

There was a curiously heavy atmosphere over

dinner that evening. Stephanie watched Rose's sour face as the housekeeper served the food and wished she hadn't bothered to come down. Even Wayne seemed unusually subdued.

Carina was brilliantly beautiful, of course, gently flirting with both men. Dean responded as though he could not help himself, his face flushed with dull red colour whenever his eyes briefly met Stephanie's. She watched him with amazement and a deep feeling of sadness. He looked guilty, like a man caught doing something he was ashamed of. She didn't understand him. He was a stranger to her, and as time passed, she too became subdued, squashed by the atmosphere around the table, greatly relieved when the meal was finished and they could retire to the open freedom of the lounge.

She had to tell him, she thought, as she drank her coffee and watched Carina capturing his attention again. She had to tell him tonight. But the opportunity did not present itself until she was on her way to her bedroom. Dean walked beside her in silence. He had not really spoken to her all evening, she realised, without surprise.

They stopped at her bedroom door. He wanted her to go inside and shut the door. He wanted to be rid of her—she could read that in his closed face and she could tell that he was trying to hide it. She felt confused and miserable.

'Dean, what's the matter?' she asked gently.

He smiled, his eyes carefully secretive. She had seen that look before. She had seen it when he had been about to gamble for high stakes and he thought she didn't know about it. 'What could be the matter?' he parried lightly.

'I want to talk to you,' she said quickly, before her courage failed her.

'What is it?' He seemed impatient.

Stephanie bit her lip, staring down the long landing. 'It would be better if we went inside,' she said, indicating her room.

Dean glanced down at his watch. 'Look, honey, can't it wait until tomorrow? I'm bushed!'

He didn't want to be bothered, she thought miserably. 'It is important,' she pressed, staring up at him.

He frowned heavily. 'We'll have breakfast together—you can talk as much as you like then,' he promised, ignoring her plea.

'Dean——' She felt desperate. Why wouldn't he talk to her now? She couldn't believe he was as tired as he claimed. His eyes were very bright, very alert, his body tense, impatient. He was lying. He was avoiding any confrontation with her. Perhaps he knew what she was going to say to him. Perhaps he wanted to put it off for as long as possible. She suddenly felt guilty for doubting him, for thinking such awful things.

'Dean——' She said his name again, a sort of plea for forgiveness. 'I. . . .'

'Tomorrow,' he cut in firmly, then briefly kissed her mouth, before opening the door of her bedroom and gently pushing her inside.

Defeated, Stephanie let herself remain silent as the door closed and she was left alone in the darkness.

That was that, she thought dully, when she knew Dean had gone. He had not wanted to talk, so they had not talked. How many times had that happened? How many times had she accepted his decisions without question?

She was crying, she realised suddenly, lifting her hand to her cheek, her fingers coming away wet with tears. If only she hadn't come to England! A little voice in her head reminded her that she would have found out that she and Dean were incompatible sooner or later, even if she had stayed at home. Better to find out before they were married. It was not much consolation, though.

She paced the room, drying her eyes. It was all such a mess, and she felt so restless and so worried that she knew she would not sleep. She *had* to speak to Dean. She stood in front of the mirror and brushed her hair, staring at her own wide-eyed reflection. She would go to his room, she would force him to listen. She left her bedroom quietly, her stomach knotted with apprehension as she crept along the silent landing to his room.

The light was on, she could see the faint crack of brightness beneath the door. Taking a deep breath, she knocked quietly, praying that he would not be annoyed. She would make him listen because they had to get everything sorted out—for both their sakes.

She waited for a minute. There was no answer. She knocked again, wondering if he had already fallen asleep, shocked to find that she was actually trembling, with the fierceness of her concentration on what she was doing. He must be there, she thought, her hand closing on the doorknob, turning it slowly, unsure that she should enter the room without being invited. But the door was swinging open and she quickly stepped inside, where the sight that met her eyes, trapped the breath in her throat, making her gasp.

On the large luxurious bed lay Dean and Carina, wrapped in each other's arms, making love.

Stephanie stared, paralysed with shock for a moment, unable to move a muscle. She felt sure she was trapped in some terrible nightmare. Dean and Carina? She couldn't believe it. Carina was going to marry Luke and Dean. . . . No wonder he had been so anxious to get rid of her this evening. No wonder he had not wanted to talk. And she had imagined that he had known what she wanted to talk about. She was such a fool!

She must have made some noise, because she saw Dean freeze, and Carina opened her eyes, the cool pale depths becoming amused as they met Stephanie's.

Dean slowly turned his head and saw her, and she could see dismay etched on every line of his flushed face. The eye contact between them seemed to bring Stephanie to her senses, and she turned on her heel and fled the room, running blindly along the thickly carpeted corridor, to her own bedroom.

Dean's shocked face was still imprinted on her mind's eye, and the total unexpected shock of what she had just witnessed numbed her brain. She wanted to feel something real—she wanted to feel something that would crack open the blank shell that was holding her thoughts prisoner. She wanted to be able to scream or cry or show any sort of reaction, but instead she found herself no more sentient than a china doll. She felt nothing—nothing at all.

Perhaps subconsciously, she had known the moment she saw Carina and Dean together, the day he arrived. There had been something between them even then, a look, an atmosphere, a communication.

She walked slowly over to the door and locked it, turning the heavy gold key—the first time she had done so since arriving here. She didn't want to be disturbed. She needed some time to think—to try and think, anyway. Her thoughts were chaotic, whirling around in useless circles, her only vision that of Carina and Dean, their naked bodies twisting together on the silken bed, the smooth brown skin of Dean's back.

Again there was no jealousy, no misery that he had cheated her with Carina. There was only shock and a numb acceptance and a vague curiosity as to why he had ever asked her to marry him.

She walked over to the long windows and opened them, watching the thin lace curtains drifting up as the wind roared in. She lit a cigarette and for the hundredth time regretted the loss of her childlike innocence. The world was a hard place. Perhaps only people like Luke and Carina and Dean survived, while she. . . . She half-smiled, she still believed in true love and fidelity.

Luke would have made love to her despite the fact that he knew she was engaged to Dean. No, that was unfair. It was he who had drawn back the day they had picnicked by the stream.

She drew deeply on her cigarette. Why on earth was she thinking of Luke, anyway, at a time like this?

She didn't hear the tapping on her door at first. Then as it grew louder and more persistent, she realised that it wasn't the wind or anything else outside. She heard Dean's urgent voice, whispering her name. She shivered, not wanting to talk to him. She moved towards the door.

'Go away,' she said quietly.

'Stephanie, let me in.' His voice was low and impatient. She couldn't imagine why he had left his bed. There was nothing he could say.

'I don't want to let you in,' she said flatly, leaning back against the hard door, eyes closed. 'Go away.' She heard him swearing under his breath and his anger confused and frightened her.

'Stephanie, open this damned door, I want to talk to you!' His voice softened then, becoming low and persuasive. 'Come on, honey, give me a chance to explain.'

Stephanie almost smiled at that. 'There's nothing to explain,' she told him quietly. 'I'm tired. I'll see you tomorrow.' She knew she was being awkward, but she couldn't have opened the door to save her life.

The situation was reversed, she thought sadly. Now Dean wanted to talk and she was refusing. It gave her no satisfaction, and she wasn't being deliberately unco-operative; she just felt raw and confused. If she let Dean in now, he would confuse her even more, brushing aside her questions, her uncertainties, pretending that everything was explainable.

He was still trying to persuade her, but she was not listening. 'We'll talk tomorrow,' she repeated when there was silence.

Dean swore again, but she knew that he was defeated, that he had given up and was going to his room. Carina would not have been pleased at his leaving her.

When she was sure he had gone, Stephanie collapsed weakly on to the bed, suddenly very tired. She sat staring blindly into thin air for long moments, before mechanically washing and undressing and climbing into bed.

Strangely, her last thought as she fell into the deep dreamless sleep of the exhausted was that she wished Luke was home.

Dean was waiting for her when she went down to breakfast the following morning. It looked arranged, she thought wryly, as she went into the dining room. Perhaps he had asked Carina and Wayne to keep out of the way. For some reason, she felt embarrassed, unwilling to face him, the episode the night before standing between them like a brick wall, blocking out all real communication.

He was sitting at the table reading a newspaper, his fair hair still wet from the shower. He looked up at Stephanie as she came in, his eyes careful and faintly guilty.

She quickly scanned the food on the long, polished sideboard and felt sick, pouring herself a cup of strong black coffee before sitting down. She sat staring down at her cup and the silence stretched between them uncomfortably. She wanted to say something, anything, just to get things started, but the words wouldn't come.

She sipped her coffee. It was too hot, scalding the roof of her mouth. She knew that Dean was watching her. What was he waiting for? Why didn't *he* say something? She felt a stab of irritation at his weakness. She was seeing a side of him she had never known, never noticed before. She had been so blind, so stupid, she could hardly believe it. She raised her eyes to meet his and saw a defensive pleading on his face. He half-smiled at her seriousness. 'Oh, Stephanie,' he said with quiet persuasion. She said nothing. She looked at him and suddenly felt calm, able to cope with anything he said. She felt older, a woman in charge of her own life.

'You don't have to explain about last night,' she began steadily, 'What I——'

'I want to,' he cut in, not giving her a chance to finish. 'You must know that Carina means nothing to me. Last night——'

'Last night, I shouldn't have barged into your room,' she interrupted, amazed that Dean could profess to feel nothing for a woman he had made love to only the night before. And she suddenly knew for certain that there had been others—many others that she had never known about. She could see it in his eyes.

'Why?' she asked quietly. 'Why, Dean?'

He shrugged, running a hand through his thick fair hair. 'She was available. She offered herself on a plate, and you don't turn down what's offered. But you've got to believe me, Stephanie, it meant nothing, and it won't happen again.'

'It has happened before, then?' she asked painfully.

He answered her with silence. She could believe that it meant nothing to him, but she could not understand it. She could not understand how he could have casual affairs with other women, when he was already engaged to her. It would have been better if they had meant something; she could have accepted that. She looked at him and inwardly sighed. He was an opportunist, a gambler. It was in his nature and he would never change.

'I can't marry you,' she told him sadly, her words dropping into the silence like cold stones.

Dean stared at her, frowning. 'Because of last night?' he demanded impatiently, incredulously.

Stephanie got to her feet and walked over to the windows, wrapping her arms around herself. 'No, not because of last night,' she said, not looking at him. 'It's nothing to do with that.'

'You're a liar.' He was behind her now. 'Stephanie, honey, don't let a stupid thing like this spoil what we have. I swear to you, it will never happen again,' he repeated, his hand on her shoulder, turning her to face him.

'It doesn't *matter*!' she told him fiercely. 'I mean that.' She was beginning to feel guilty even though she knew he was making promises he would be unable to keep, given the kind of opportunity Carina had given him last night. He was so charming, so sincere, so sorry.

'Then what the hell is it?' he demanded roughly.

She nervously licked her lips. 'I've known that I can't marry you for quite a while. That's what I wanted to talk to you about, last night.' She paused, searching for the right words, hating what she was doing. 'Oh, Dean, can't you see? We love each other as friends, but if we married, it would be a disaster, it wouldn't last five minutes. You must know that in your heart.'

Dean stared at her as though seeing her for the very

first time. 'You're talking bloody rubbish,' he said coldly, all persuasive charm leaving him, as anger hardened his face. 'What's the matter with you, anyway? A lousy one-night stand and you want to break off our engagement? Everything's over?'

Stephanie felt her eyes filling with tears, hurt by his sudden anger.

'Why don't you listen to me?' she demanded shakily. 'And stop treating me like a child! I *can't* marry you. We don't love each other enough, we don't love each other the right way.'

'No?' His mouth twisted with scorn, his hands tightening on her shoulders, hurting her uncaringly, in anger. 'What the hell do you know about love, anyway? I want you, I've wanted you for years, and I'm going to have you.' He gritted furiously. 'We've been playing your games for far too long!'

'Dean. . . . Dean, please. . . .' Stephanie felt frightened of him for the first time in her life. She hadn't realised that breaking off their engagement would be such a blow to his pride. He didn't love her, she knew that for certain now. He wanted her, and she saw the ruthlessness beneath the charming mask.

'Please?' he laughed mockingly. 'You want out? It's not going to be that easy, honey.'

'There was someone else!' she shouted in desperation. 'I let him . . . kiss me . . . it made me realise. . . .'

'Another man?' Dean's eyes were dangerous, as he saw his prize slipping away from him.

Stephanie nodded, her eyes enormous, and he swore violently. 'You bloody little hypocrite!' he snapped savagely. 'Well, that's it, we're finished. I'm the one who wants out.'

She didn't realise his intention until his mouth forced her lips apart. It was a brutal, punishing kiss, totally devoid of tenderness. She fought him, beating at his chest with small clenched fists, fearful of the contemptuous lust in his mouth, in his hands.

At last she managed to tear her mouth from beneath his. 'No, Dean, please don't. . . .' Her voice was shaking badly.

'You heard the lady, Sangster, don't.' Luke's cool hard voice broke between them, and Stephanie had never felt more relieved to see him. Dean's body stiffened and she looked up over his shoulder to see Luke in the doorway, his eyes bleak, his mouth tight with anger.

'Mind your own damn business, Baroda!' Dean snapped, not turning, still staring at Stephanie, his breath coming harshly, his eyes still glazed with lust.

'It is my business,' Luke replied in a smooth icy voice. 'Let her go.'

Stephanie could hear the threat of violence in his cold words. Dean heard it too. She saw his face change, his hands dropping from her.

'I think I'm beginning to understand,' he said unpleasantly, his meaning clear.

Luke stepped into the room and Stephanie looked at him, her eyes pleading. She didn't think she could bear any more trouble. Her knees felt like jelly, her heart was pounding suffocatingly.

Dean turned then, sensing and reacting to the threat of violence emanating from Luke. He looked at them both once, before striding from the room without a word.

Stephanie stared after him, shaking like a leaf. Luke watched her, his eyes very dark, his mouth still tight and angry.

'Oh God!' she whispered, pressing a hand to the pulse beating so hurriedly in her throat. 'What have I done?'

'What have you done?' he asked coolly, moving towards her.

She looked at him, staring into his face, taking in the taut bones, the dark green of his eyes, the firm strength of his mouth.

'I've broken off my engagement,' she told him in a trembling voice.

'Stephanie——' His voice was low and gentle. He reached out his hand to touch her cheek, but she shrank away in panic.

'Don't touch me!' she whispered, irrationally blaming him, because he had sewn the first seeds of doubt about Dean in her mind. 'I couldn't bear it!'

Luke's face hardened, becoming blank, shuttered, and his hand dropped.

'The solicitors will be here at noon,' he reminded her in a clipped voice.

Stephanie smiled hysterically. 'I'd forgotten all about that,' she said, with wild laughter in her voice, and turning away from him, ran from the room to find some privacy, where she could try and make some sense of what had just happened.

CHAPTER EIGHT

By the time Stephanie got back to the house after a long walk along the cliffs, it was eleven o'clock. She had just enough time to grab a cup of coffee and change before the solicitors arrived.

Unfortunately, Carina was in the dining room. Stephanie sighed.

'Good morning,' she said with polite dismay, as she reached for the coffee pot.

Carina smiled that secretive acid smile that Stephanie hated. 'Good morning, darling. I'm glad I've caught you—I wanted a word before the solicitors arrived.'

Stephanie glanced at her watch. 'You'll have to be quick,' she said coolly, 'I've a lot to do.'

For some reason she was no longer intimidated by Carina, even though she saw the flash of irritation in her half-sister's eyes.

'In that case, I'll come straight to the point. It's about last night. . . .' Stephanie half-smiled. She felt very much calmer since her walk. Outside, by the crashing sea, it was easier to see things in perspective, it was easier to work things out. She wondered what Carina would say.

'What about last night?' Carina queried obtusely, sipping her coffee quite calmly.

'Well. . . .' Carina paused delicately. 'Well, I think I probably owe you an explanation.'

'I'm listening,' Stephanie felt surprised. 'But I ought to tell you that I broke off my engagement to Dean this morning—so really explanations are unnecessary.'

134

Carina stared at her, obviously surprised by the news. 'Rather drastic, isn't it, darling? He is a very attractive young man, after all.'

'If you find him that attractive, you're welcome to him,' Stephanie said flatly, wondering how she could sit here drinking coffee and talking about Dean so coolly. 'Although I suppose I'm rather late in making that offer.'

Carina had the grace to look uncomfortable. 'It was only a one-night stand, darling, it certainly doesn't mean anything.'

Stephanie shrugged. 'That's what Dean said, but the point is that he slept with you when he was supposed to be engaged to me.' A thought struck her. 'Will you tell Luke?'

Carina's eyes hardened. 'Will you?'

'It's none of my business.'

The older girl smiled. 'Perhaps that *was* in the back of my mind. I want to make him jealous—it might make him sit up and take notice.'

'Is he neglecting you?' Stephanie asked sweetly, silently marvelling at Carina's selfish motives. Had she really slept with Dean just to make Luke jealous? It was unbelievable! And if Stephanie knew Luke at all, she felt sure that the plan wouldn't work.

Carina ignored the question, smoothing back her raven hair. 'Whatever you think, Stephanie, I don't want to be the cause of your broken engagement. It really was a spur-of-the-moment thing. I suppose I was bored, what with Luke being away.'

'What about Wayne?' Stephanie asked curiously.

'Wayne bores me as well,' said Carina with languid candour.

He, too, had been used, Stephanie realised. Probably a brief affair, probably on another occasion when Luke was away. The trouble was that Wayne still wanted Carina. Stephanie had seen it in his eyes, heard it in his voice.

It was all so pointless, so destructive. How could Luke love her? Why was he going to marry her?

She sighed. It would be so easy to let Carina think it was her fault the engagement was broken, it would be easy to blame her, but Stephanie couldn't bring herself to do it.

'Don't worry,' she said wryly. 'I decided to break off the engagement long before last night. Your conscience can be clear.'

Carina smiled. 'Well, that's a relief. Anybody else in mind?'

They both knew she was speaking of Luke, both remembering Carina's warning. What would her half-sister say, Stephanie wondered, if she told her that two could play at that game, and that Luke was the next man on her list? She doubted that Carina would be pleased.

'Wouldn't you like to know?' Stephanie finished the last mouthful of her coffee and got hastily to her feet, trying to hide the revealing colour in her cheeks that the very thought of Luke had brought.

'I've got to change,' she said, and left the room, marvelling, as she made her way upstairs, how impossible it was to stay annoyed with Carina for very long.

Even though she knew that Carina was a cold, hard, self-obsessed bitch, she still had a grudging fondness for her. Even though she instinctively knew that Carina had taken the initiative in her brief affair with Dean, Stephanie couldn't rustle up any resentment towards her.

And Luke? she asked herself wryly; how do you feel about Carina and Luke?

It was there again, that nagging pain in the region of

her heart. A pain that she didn't want to—didn't dare to examine too closely. That seemed to be the point where she lost any fondness she had for Carina, whenever she thought of her with Luke.

None of it matters, she thought fiercely, as she walked into her bedroom. After this meeting, I can leave. Which only left the question, where would she go?

She washed and changed into a pale green silk suit with a contrasting blouse. She looked cool and businesslike, she thought, as she brushed her hair in front of the mirror. The suit was beautifully cut, the flaring hemline swinging softly around her slim legs. She looked good, and she needed the confidence that knowledge gave her.

It was ten to twelve as she strolled downstairs to the library where the meeting was to take place. There was no sign of Dean anywhere, but Stephanie wanted to get the meeting over with before facing him again. Tentatively pushing open the heavy library door, she saw Luke, Carina and two men inside.

Luke came towards her immediately. 'Come in.' He smiled slightly. She let him take her arm, despite Carina's piercing glance, her heart pounding at his touch. He was wearing an expensively cut dark suit, that gave him a remote air of power, of success.

'Would you like a drink?' He looked down at her, his narrowed glance searching, and as she raised her eyes to his, a fierce awareness ran between them.

Stephanie lowered her head confusedly. 'A small sherry, please.'

She was introduced to the two solicitors, Mr Taborn, old and portly and probably pompous, his thin white hair barely framing his round, red face, and Mr Wood, thin-faced and younger and very much more slick, as he eyed Stephanie appreciatively.

Carina looked bored and very beautiful, languorously curled up in a leather chair near the open fire. And Stephanie watched Luke, almost unaware she was doing so. She slowly sipped her sherry and stared at his hard-boned, serious face, at his beautifully moulded mouth, unable to drag her gaze away. She watched him move with that sleek, panther-like grace, watched the lazy effortless charm in his eyes as he talked, and felt herself falling into the web of his attraction, his magnificence.

Finally they all sat around the large oak table, the solicitors pulling sheaves of paper out of leather attache cases. Mr Taborn asked Luke to stay.

It was all very serious, the atmosphere heavy, telling of bad news to come. And when it did come, Stephanie was stunned.

Mr Taborn's droning voice hit her like sharp stones. Luke had tried to prepare her, she realised, he had tried to warn her, but it was still a terrible shock.

Her father had died penniless—worse than penniless, in debt for many thousands of pounds that he had embezzled from Luke's hotels while in Luke's employ. There was no doubt, it was a matter of record. The solicitor read a letter written by Stephanie's father just before his death, confessing the theft.

Stephanie couldn't believe it, couldn't take it in, the amount was so terrifyingly large. She hadn't known her father at all.

'You knew,' she said, staring at Luke.

'Yes, I knew,' he confirmed coolly, 'But you can rest assured that I don't intend to take the matter any further.'

The solicitors were very surprised, but Luke was adamant. He had written the money off; he and Stephanie's father had been friends. Stephanie watched him as he smiled at Carina, and her heart twisted. He was doing it all for Carina. He must love her very much, she thought defeatedly, and turned away.

'What happened to all the money?' Carina asked curiously.

Mr Taborn consulted the papers in front of him. 'The money was invested in a company that went bankrupt. I have the name here ... Island Holdings——'

Stephanie ceased to listen at that second, her face draining of all colour, unaware that Luke was watching her closely. Mr Taborn's voice receded into her consciousness as she tried to remember Island Holdings.

Of course! She had heard Camil mention it one day when she had been in Dean's office, waiting for him to take her to lunch. She forced herself to remember the conversation, pulling it from the back of her mind. She felt almost sure that Dean owned that company, and if he did ... the implications were overwhelmingly horrifying.

She sat in silence, trying to work it all out, totally unaware of the other people in the room. Had Dean known her father? What was the link between them? And if Dean had been working with her father, why hadn't he ever mentioned it? She suddenly remembered something Luke had said about a photograph. She looked at him. He looked calm, unsurprised, chatting to Mr Wood. He knew what was going on. He knew it all, and had told nobody.

The will was read next. Everything went to Carina, as expected, except for a sealed letter and a gold watch for Stephanie, which she took with tear-filled eyes, knowing that she wouldn't read the letter until later when she was alone.

The rest of the meeting passed in a haze. She heard

nothing of what was being said, and escaped as soon as she could, glad to get away, uncaring that Luke's narrowed eyes followed her as she abruptly left the room.

She had to know the truth, and Dean seemed to hold the key. Fortunately his hired car was still outside, and she checked the downstairs rooms before running upstairs. She knocked on his bedroom door and heard his brief, brusque command to come in.

He was on the telephone, a suitcase open on the bed, filled with clothes. He was leaving.

Stephanie stood by the window, not listening to him talking on the phone, gripped with a haunting sadness. He had not looked pleased to see her as she came in. Had he been expecting Carina?

She looked down at the sapphire ring on her finger and quickly pulled it off. She had been hopelessly naïve to think that they could still be friends.

Outside, the horizon was a grey blur, two toy-sized ships static against the sky. Deep in her heart she had known that they were not right for each other long before leaving the island. That was why she had been so reluctant to name the wedding day. It was just so sad that it had come to this, that it should end this way. But, however unpleasant, she had to know the truth about her father before Dean walked out of her life for ever.

She heard the faint click of the receiver being replaced, but couldn't turn round. She was suddenly afraid of what she had done, of what she might hear.

'What do you want?' Dean's impatient voice turned her head.

'You're leaving,' she said quietly.

'There's not a hell of a lot to stay for, is there?'

It was as though she wasn't there. He carried on flinging things into the suitcase, unfolded.

'I didn't want it to end this way,' she said miserably.

Dean laughed humourlessly. 'I'd never have guessed.' He had not looked at her once.

'I want us to be friends. There's so much we've shared in the past—we grew up together!' she cried, because she felt so lonely. Without Dean she would be totally alone in the world.

He looked at her then, his blue eyes furious, contemptuous. 'That's a tall order, honey,' he said, snapping shut the locks on his suitcase.

'I know.' Stephanie bowed her head. Of course, she was asking too much.

'With me, it's all or nothing—that's how I run my life,' Dean told her, 'and I'm certainly not interested in Baroda's cast-offs.'

Stephanie gasped. 'You know very well that it's not like that!'

Dean's eyes were cynical. 'No?'

'No!'

'Well, let's just forget it, huh? I'm really not that interested.' He glanced at the gold watch on his wrist. 'My plane leaves in one and a half hours' time. I've got to be going.'

He didn't care at all; she could see that in his face. He had written her off in much the same way that Luke had written off the embezzled money. It didn't matter.

'Why did you ever ask me to marry you?' she asked painfully, because that was the one thing she couldn't understand.

Dean shrugged into his jacket, obviously impatient to get away. 'What is this—a third degree? Are you deaf? I've got a plane to catch.'

'Why?' she persisted stubbornly.

Standing still at last, he said, 'I wanted you because you were untouched, you'd always been mine. No other man had been near you.' There was an ugliness in his face, in his voice as he spoke, an ugliness and a brutal possessiveness that frightened her.

Stephanie shook her head in amazement. It was perfectly all right for him to have as many affairs as he liked, but she had to be untouched! It was incredible—all the more incredible because she had been totally unware of his motives, of what had been going on right under her nose. He had never loved her; she knew that for certain now.

'Thanks for telling me,' she managed steadily.

'Is that all? Can I go now?' There was a sarcastic edge to his voice. He was treating her as he treated his employees at the casino.

'There is just one more thing——' Stephanie began.

'What is it, now?'

'Island Holdings is your company, isn't it?'

Dean smiled, but she saw the wariness in his eyes. 'You tell me.'

'The solicitors told me that my father embezzled thousands of pounds from Luke. He invested the money in a company called Island Holdings.'

'So?' Dean's expression was unpleasant.

'So, it's *your* company, isn't it?'

'Yes, it is, but what does that prove?'

Stephanie could hardly believe his coldness. 'Did you know my father?' she demanded unsteadily.

'Yes, I knew him.' It was not an admission, more a cool statement of unimportant fact.

'Why didn't you tell me?' She suddenly felt very unsure of herself. She could feel the tears blocking her throat.

'Look, honey, I really have to go.' Dean was picking up his case, moving towards the door.

'*Why?*' she demanded again, and moved after him, grasping his arm.

He shook her off, irritation in every line of his body. 'We both knew that I'd be a bloody fool to say anything else—so let's just leave it,' he said coldly, opening the door.

Terribly hurt, Stephanie held out the sapphire engagement ring. 'This is yours,' she said, in a voice shaking with tears.

'Keep it,' came the uncaring reply. 'You might need it when Baroda gets tired of you.'

Then he was gone, without so much as a backwards glance. Gone for ever.

She felt the tears pouring down her face. She felt utterly desolate—partly because of what Dean had done and partly because she felt she could not blame him for being angry. She ripped open the letter from her father. It was brief. He loved her and regretted the lack of contact between them. Too late, too late.

Needing to get out of the room, out of the house, Stephanie hurried downstairs, still clutching the sapphire ring, and outside.

She ran towards the cliffs, unaware that the rain was starting, noticing only that Dean's hired car was gone. She scrambled down the cliff path to the bay, uncaring that the sharp stones grazed her legs when she stumbled and tore at the hem of her silk skirt, only the screaming of the gulls filling her head. The sea was rough and grey, the waves edged with white. She stood at the angry water's edge and, lifting her arm, threw the ring with all her strength into the sea. Now it was ended once and for all.

'It will only get washed up again.' The low, cool voice behind her made her jump. It was Luke. He had followed her again.

'I hope it brings the finder more happiness than it brought me,' Stephanie said bitterly, not turning round, only just realising that she was soaked through.

It was raining heavily now, the thin silk of her suit was clinging revealingly to every curve of her body, her wet hair was plastered to her small head.

'Heartbroken?' Luke queried sardonically.

'Maybe.' She wished he would go away.

'I don't believe you.' There was laughter in his voice.

'He's gone.' She sounded lost.

'What did you expect?' She got the impression that he was angry with her.

'That must be my trouble,' she said wryly. 'I obviously do expect too much.'

'You're feeling sorry for yourself, that's all.' The tenderness in his voice shuddered through her.

She felt raw and very vulnerable, still unable to cope with Dean's leaving, with everything that had happened in this one crazy day. Her whole life had been turned upside down within the space of twenty-four hours and it had left her feeling that she had no solid ground beneath her feet. One small step in the wrong direction could leave her falling into some dark, unknown precipice, because all the solid reliable things in her life had been torn away.

'Of course I'm feeling sorry for myself!' she retorted, trying to ignore the effect he was having on her. 'It's a luxury I can't often afford.'

Luke was silent—so silent she thought he might have gone, so that when his hand touched her shoulder, she trembled violently, turning to him.

The furious roar of the sea, the screeching of the gulls and the howling wind filled the silence between them, leaving it more empty, more nerve-racking. He was as wet as she was, she noticed absently, the fine cotton shirt he wore, stuck fast to the wide muscular line of his shoulders.

It was darker now as they stood face to face on the

tiny landlocked beach. She looked into the brooding darkness of his eyes and could not say a word.

'The tide is coming in,' he told her, his green eyes holding hers.

'Tell me about my father and Dean,' Stephanie said quietly.

'Ask Sangster,' said Luke, a muscle moving spasmodically in his jaw.

'I did, but he wouldn't tell me.' Her eyes pleaded, unconsciously beautiful. 'You know. Please tell me!'

He didn't want to, she could see that as he remained silent.

'Please!' she repeated urgently. 'I have to know—it's driving me mad!'

Luke stared down at her for a moment and she couldn't tell what he was thinking.

'Stephanie——' he began.

'I know it's not your responsibility, but you're the only other person who knows,' she cut in desperately.

'Okay.' He smiled slightly at her sweetness. 'You recognised the company name?'

'Yes, one of Dean's companies.' She felt almost as though she was betraying him—and herself.

'Apparently your father met Sangster when he was in London on business. Your father was anxious to re-establish contact with you, but he was reluctant to get in touch with you directly, after so many years of silence. Sangster gave him a photograph of you,' Luke revealed in clipped tones.

Stephanie's eyes filled with sad tears. 'He should have got in touch with *me*,' she said shakily.

'He was proud and stubborn and he still felt very bitter about the divorce,' Luke explained gently, watching her. 'Perhaps he was afraid you would reject him. I think he wanted to find out about you first.'

Stephanie thought about that, and it made her hurt

even more because Dean had never said a word about it. She hadn't received the slightest hint, and now it was too late.

'And the money?' she asked, wanting to know it all.

Luke shrugged restlessly. 'I had no idea until the auditors went in. You have to understand that in a lot of ways your father was very like Sangster. He was an opportunist, he liked taking risks. Sangster offered him an easy way to make a great deal of money. He would have been set up for life. And it would have worked—the money he took from the hotels would have been replaced before anyone noticed it was missing, had Sangster's company not gone to the wall.' His voice was cool and calm, but Stephanie could see the anger in his eyes.

'And that's it?'

'That's it.'

He had made it easy for her, she realised with a rush of gratitude. He could have said a lot more, but he had given her only the cold hard facts, allowing her to place her own interpretation on them.

'But isn't ... isn't what Dean did illegal?' she queried.

Luke shook his head. 'He's clever, and believe me, if there was any way I could get him into court, I would.'

'But what about. . . .?' Stephanie stopped, biting her lip savagely.

'Him and Carina?' Luke hazarded calmly.

'You know?' She was astonished.

'I guessed.' He didn't sound as though he cared one way or the other.

'I'm glad you stepped in this morning,' she said, shivering at the very remembrance of it.

Luke smiled. 'At the beginning, I suspected you might be involved in Sangster's shady dealings.'

Stephanie stared at him, wide-eyed. She couldn't blame him for that. 'Never!' she said emphatically.

'I know that now—I knew the moment I met you.' His voice became very low. 'You're so innocent.'

She flushed. Stupid, was the word she would have used. She thought back and realised that he had been testing her. *He* was the clever one. She had the feeling that he had outwitted them all.

'Thank you for not taking it any further,' she said quietly.

'I liked your father—and there's no reason for the people who are left to suffer. It's only money, after all,' said Luke with a faint shrug of his shoulders.

He meant Carina, of course. She turned back towards the sea, which had swallowed up at least a foot more of the beach. The tide was coming fast.

Maybe Luke was right; maybe she had been attracted to Dean because he so resembled her father. If it was true, it had not been a conscious thing. When she was a child, Dean had been a father/brother figure to her. She had always turned to him for protection, had always taken her problems to him. And if that was so, if she had subconsciously needed him as a substitute father, their relationship had been doomed right from the beginning.

She felt the warm rain on her face. She did not want to go back to the house, she wanted to stay here for a while.

'Thanks for telling me,' she said over her shoulder.

Luke did not answer. 'What will you do?' he asked, watching her vulnerable profile.

'I'm leaving,' she told him shortly.

'Back home?' His voice was harsh.

'No, no, not for a while, anyway. I don't know—the world is my oyster.' Her voice broke on the last word, but she stiffened her shoulders and swallowed back the tears, not wanting to reveal her weakness.

'You can stay here as long as you like,' he told her, still watching her. She thought of him with Carina and her heart twisted.

'I don't want to stay here. I hate this place!' she retorted emotionally.

'Do you think I'm just going to let you walk away?' Luke asked expressionlessly.

'You can't stop me,' she told him steadily. She looked at him in surprise, her breath catching at the magnificent power of his body, at the dark hair plastered against his skull, throwing the stark bones of his face into sharp relief.

'You're a fool if you really think that,' he said, his mouth twisting harshly. 'I still want you, Stephanie. The only difference is that Sangster is now out of the running and you're a free woman.' His voice had become deeper, low and possessive.

Stephanie stared at him wildly; her heart jumping into her throat, her legs weakening in response to the sensual threat of his words. She *had* to fight him, because he was practically engaged to her half-sister, and although nobody else at the house seemed to care about casual affairs, she did.

She wanted Luke—there was no point in denying that, but if she became his lover, he would be a part of her for ever. For her it would mean everything, whereas for him, as for Carina and Dean and Wayne, it would be nothing more than a passing pleasure, a satisfaction of his needs.

'Yes, I'm free,' she said angrily. 'Free to say no, which is what I'm saying to you. I don't want you!'

'Is that so?' drawled Luke, his dark gaze sliding down her body in slow masculine appraisal, over every curve visible beneath the soaking silk.

'It's so!' she snapped, and turned away from him, walking stiffly back up a beach that was getting smaller by the minute now. It was darker too, and the warm rain was still lashing down, ignored by both of them.

Luke was behind her in a split second, and pulled her round to face him, his mouth tight with anger, eyes burning. Without a word, he tangled a hand in her wet hair, pulling back her head to expose her mouth, the white line of her throat.

'I've waited too long for you,' he told her, his cool clean breath fanning her cheek.

'You'll wait for ever! Let me go—I don't want you!' Stephanie spat, fighting him and fighting herself and finding it almost impossible.

A faint smile touched the corners of Luke's mouth. 'I can prove you a liar,' he murmured, his smoky gaze fixed on the gentle outline of her face. 'And the challenge is irresistible.'

His mouth touched hers with anger and she knew that her insults had hit home. But her momentary awareness was soon drowned beneath the hungry demand of his lips.

'No, Luke, no. . . .' she murmured, under the pressure of his kiss, splaying her hands against his hard chest, trying to push him away.

He was far too strong for her and he was holding her too tightly, almost cruelly, the long fingers tangled in her hair, holding her still beneath the drugging touch of his mouth. All her fierce resistance seemed to melt into nothing as she heard him groaning softly and his mouth became gentle, more intimate, his tongue tracing the outline of her parted lips. His hand left her hair to slide lower, down the curve of her spine to mould her even closer to the powerful strength of his body. She could feel the heat in him, the hard need, and she shivered, trembling violently against him in defeat, her heart pounding as though it would burst.

Luke felt the restless shivering of her body and lifted his dark head. He looked into her eyes, his own heavy, black with a desire he could not conceal. Stephanie saw that desire and a weak ache of triumph shot through her. She stared at him as though in a trance, her own tongue now tracing the bruised responsive softness of her lips in unknowing provocation.

'Oh God, Stephanie,' Luke said deeply, 'hold me. I want to feel your arms around me.'

She couldn't fight the feelings he was arousing in her, they were too deep, unleashing a need in her she had not known existed. And before she realised what she was doing, her hands were sliding to his powerful shoulders, stroking the tensed muscles her fingers remembered so well. Her mouth met his again, soft and parted, silently and sweetly offering him the passion he had aroused, the passion he demanded.

She felt the stillness of surprise in him for a second, then he groaned low in his throat, his arms tightened around her, their mouths fusing with a desire, a wildness that shook them both with its ferocious sweetness. His mouth trailed fire across her throat, his hands deftly pushing the silk from her shoulders, her breasts, exposing her bare wet skin to his touch.

The tide was rolling in faster, lapping at their feet and its cold threat brought Stephanie to her senses. What was she doing, allowing Luke to make love to her like this? Her moaning pleasure died, shrivelling instantly, and she pushed at his unyielding chest.

'Luke—the tide.'

He lifted his head reluctantly and smiled down into her glazed frightened eyes, his breathing harsh and uneven. In silence, he took her hand, and they climbed the path back to the house.

Stephanie was glad he was silent. She thought she

would probably curl up with embarrassment if he spoke and she knew he was aware of that.

As they reached the house, she said, too sharply, 'I *am* leaving tomorrow.'

Luke turned his head and looked at her, totally in control of himself, as though nothing at all had happened on the beach. And there was a tautness around his mouth as he said, 'Why are you telling me?'

She swallowed painfully, her mind blank for a second. She had been telling herself as well. She had to get away from him before it was too late, before . . . before she fell in love with him. If she went inside with him now, she would end up in his bed tonight.

'Why, Stephanie?' Luke persisted coolly. He was violently angry and she couldn't look at him, afraid of what he might read in her eyes.

'There's nothing to stay for,' she said clearly. 'Nothing at all.'

She felt him stiffen beside her, well aware of what she was doing. But instead of destroying her with cold words, as she expected, he stared down at her profile for a second or two longer, then left her in silence. He disappeared inside the house, and the door slammed behind him, leaving her alone, as she had wanted, but aching with regret.

CHAPTER NINE

CANNES was very, very hot, and madly busy, it being the height of the tourist season.

It was Stephanie's afternoon off and she was lying on the Croisette beach improving her suntan and pretending to read the French novel she had brought with her. The relentless sun beat down on her back, relaxing her, and she closed her eyes. It was wonderful to relax and do nothing. The restaurant had been so busy over the past couple of days, she hadn't had a minute to breathe, and for some reason she had not been sleeping well at all.

She opened her eyes again, on a sigh, and adjusted her sunglasses, noticing that a tanned young man further up the beach was staring fixedly at her. She frowned slightly and ignored him. If he approached her, she would casually freeze him off—she'd had plenty of practice at that since arriving in Cannes!

It was now three weeks since she had left Luke's house by the sea. She had gone, as promised, the morning after he had tried to make love to her on the beach.

The evening before she left, Luke had not been at dinner. Carina's eyes had been wary and very suspicious over the meal, as though she knew what had happened. But Stephanie had been uncaring, racking her brains for somewhere to go.

Then she had remembered her old school friend Françoise Massin, who had left Moahu with her parents to go back to France soon after both girls left school. Stephanie still wrote to Françoise and they were still fairly close. That was it—problem solved! She would go to France, stay in a hotel if Françoise could not put her up.

After dinner, Stephanie had escaped early and sat by the phone making plans.

Françoise was delighted to hear from her. Of course she could come over and stay—they always needed help in the restaurant-bar they owned. She was very welcome. It had been a great relief, and Stephanie had been genuinely thrilled at the thought of seeing Françoise again.

Next, she had booked her flight for mid-morning the following day, then had telephoned Connie to explain her plans. Connie had been very curious, having already heard the gossip that her engagement to Dean was broken off, but Stephanie had been unable to talk about it, promising to write and explain everything as soon as she got to Cannes.

Then there had been packing, and arranging for a taxi to pick her up early the following morning.

Carina had not seemed sorry to find out that she was leaving. 'Cannes? Very nice, darling,' she had said casually. 'Take care of yourself—we'll probably meet again some time.'

Stephanie had smiled, 'I hope so.' She had meant it. She still regretted the fact that she and Carina had not been friends.

Wayne had seemed genuinely sad to hear of her departure. 'I'll miss you,' he had told her, kissing her cheek. 'You livened the place up a bit.'

'Let's keep in touch.' She had grown fond of him, she had realised as she suggested it. He was like a brother.

She had not seen Luke, she hadn't had the courage to seek him out, and he had made no move to see her.

When she left the next day, the depth of her sadness

at leaving the house had shocked her. She felt desolate at the thought of never seeing Luke again, even though they had parted in anger.

Françoise and her brother, Philippe, met her at Nice airport. It was good to see Françoise again, and Philippe was as charming and as friendly as Stephanie remembered. She was tired after an almost sleepless night and in consequence did not fully appreciate the beautiful views on the ride to Cannes.

The restaurant-bar Philippe owned was in the centre of town, near the sea-front, and Françoise worked and lived there with him, their parents having moved to Paris two years before. Stephanie's room was pleasantly large with a plant-filled balcony overlooking the road. There was a brass bed and dark wooden furniture.

At dinner that first night, she told them both that she would be looking for a job, and Philippe immediately offered her one in the restaurant. He explained that they needed all the help they could get at the height of the season.

Philippe was tall and olive-skinned with tawny hair that fell over his forehead, and a thin face. He was attracted to her, she could see that every time he looked at her, but she was deliberately ignoring it. She had only just managed to get her thoughts sorted out about Dean and her father, and Luke filled all her senses, day and night. She could not get him out of her mind, only glad that she had got away before it was too late.

So, on her second day in Cannes, she began to work in the restaurant, despite Françoise's protests that she was on holiday and should spend at least a week sightseeing and sunbathing. It was hard, busy work and Stephanie was thankful, because it took her mind off Luke. She picked up the work easily, her fluency in French being a great help. And she had to admit that she was enjoying it.

Françoise was a good friend, despite the fact that they hadn't seen each other for years, and they got on well, laughing whenever they were together. And Stephanie liked Cannes and was faintly amused by the opulent wealth on display here, loving the sun and the easy holiday atmosphere.

She rolled on to her back and glanced at her watch. It was five o'clock, time she was getting back to help with the evening work. She collected her bag and slipped on the brightly-coloured sarong she had brought with her, then left the beach, feeling the eyes of the young man who had been staring at her so blatantly following her every inch of the way. Then she crossed the Boulevard de la Croisette, walking under the shady palm trees, stopping to glance in one or two shop windows on her way back to the restaurant.

Françoise was behind the bar when she arrived. 'Nice afternoon?' the French girl asked with a smile, flicking back her waist-length black hair.

'I just lay on the beach,' Stephanie admitted ruefully, 'doing absolutely nothing.'

'Good for you!' Françoise carried on with her task of counting glasses.

The room was dim, the light filtering through shuttered blinds. Empty like this, it held a charm that could only be French.

'I'll take a quick shower, then I'll give you a hand,' Stephanie promised, the bead curtains rustling musically as she pushed through them.

Her room was dark and cool and she kicked off her sandals, cooling her feet on the tile floor as she walked into the shower. She dried and plaited her hair, then dressed in green cotton trousers and a matching short-sleeved blouse, before making her way back downstairs to help Françoise set the tables.

'What's the matter?' she asked her friend, noticing her frown of concentration as they worked. Françoise lifted her shoulders in a characteristic shrug.

'Oh, it's Claude. He phoned before to say that he'll be delayed for a further two days, and I'm missing him like mad!'

Françoise was having a passionate affair with the owner of an antique shop. He had been away for weeks on a buying trip. They would probably marry eventually, Françoise confided to Stephanie, but for the moment they were enjoying their affair. Françoise was supremely happy, Stephanie could see her face lighting up whenever she thought of Claude, her dark eyes radiant.

'Two days will pass quickly, you'll see,' she promised sympathetically.

'It might as well be two weeks,' Françoise replied mournfully, 'I thought he would be back tonight.'

Philippe wandered in as they were chatting. 'Everything in order?' His dark eyes rested on Stephanie.

'What else?' Françoise replied laughingly. 'Isn't everything always in order?'

And when she disappeared into the kitchens to check the menus with the chef, Philippe said to Stephanie, 'Have dinner with me this week?'

Stephanie smiled, embarrassed. 'I'll be working here,' she protested lightly, hoping that he wouldn't push it.

'Nicolas and Jeanne will take over for one evening,' he told her calmly. 'We could dance—I know a wonderful place on the old harbour—the fish there is fantastic. I know you would like it.'

He was serious, and her heart sank as she saw that,

because she liked him. 'What would Françoise say?' she parried, still smiling.

'It is not Françoise's business.'

'I'll think about it,' she promised, because she didn't have the heart to turn him down flat, not when he had been so kind to her.

'I'll keep on asking you until you say yes,' he assured her, meaning it, his smile warm with charm.

Stephanie smiled in silence and turned back to her work, wondering what on earth she would do if he did.

The restaurant was packed again that evening, and working behind the bar, Stephanie was rushed off her feet. She prepared and served drinks automatically, fending off passes of all types from male customers, as usual, watching Françoise, in her fashionable white shorts, doing the same. It was so predictable it was funny, and the two girls shared jokes about it all evening.

Philippe hurried over to the bar, halfway through the evening, obviously flustered, to order extra special treatment for a party that had just come in—a Hollywood film star and his entourage.

It was quite usual in Cannes, Stephanie had already been warned, and she spent the next couple of hours mixing cocktails and serving wine and champagne to the party, who became louder and drunker as the evening passed.

After a much-needed break and something to eat in the kitchens at about nine-thirty, she returned to the bar refreshed. It was still crowded, so busy now that she hardly had time to look at the customers she was serving. She moved towards the figure of a man seated on one of the high, plushly-upholstered wooden bar stools.

'*Monsieur?*' she murmured, clearing away empty glasses, not looking at him.

'Scotch, neat.' The deep cool voice jerked her head up in amazement, her heart thudding. It was Luke, his eyes flaming with anger.

'Scotch,' Stephanie repeated inanely, still incredibly shocked to see him. He nodded briskly, and her hands trembled as she served him.

It was like a dream. He had been constantly in her thoughts since she left England. How had he known where to find her? What was he doing here, anyway?

She glanced at him from beneath her lashes. He looked powerful and menacing, his anger—anger that she could not understand—almost tangible. He was wearing jeans and a green checked shirt, and even dressed so casually, he was still the most devastatingly attractive man in the place.

Luckily, because they were so busy, she could move away as soon as she had served him. He had said nothing remotely personal to her. To a third person looking on, there was no evidence that they were anything other than strangers, Stephanie reflected miserably. But she felt his blank eyes following every move she made, as she served the other customers.

He did not take his eyes off her for a second, and in consequence, she became flushed and clumsy, actually dropping two glasses and smashing them, she was so aware of him. She had to serve him a number of times, and each time he was silent, and she could find no courage to speak to him.

'What's the matter?' Françoise asked perceptively, as she waited at the bar for a bottle of wine for one of the customers at a table. 'Is it too much for you?'

'Of course not.' Stephanie tried to smile, but failed miserably. 'Probably too much sun on the beach this afternoon.' It was a poor lie, but Françoise, sensing that she did not want to talk, shrugged and dropped the subject.

'Have you seen that gorgeous man sitting at the bar? The one in the green shirt?'

She meant Luke, and Stephanie's colour rose. 'Yes, I've seen him,' she said shortly, dismissively.

'Mm.' Françoise was staring at him openly, ignoring Stephanie's lack of interest, her eyes dreaming. 'That's quite a man *and*, he's alone.' She sounded as though she was talking about some kind of god, and Stephanie snorted.

'You're spoken for,' she reminded her friend with a smile.

'Even so——' Françoise said wistfully. 'Green eyes—they send shivers down my spine. He's fantastic!'

Stephanie raised her eyes towards the ceiling. 'You're mad,' she said firmly, because Françoise was echoing her own thoughts. 'Here's your wine.'

And so the time passed, Luke watching her in brooding silence as she dashed around working. She watched him too—covertly. She watched him smoking, watched him drinking Scotch, her face very flushed and a restless shivering in her body. She wanted to know what on earth he was doing in Cannes, but she didn't dare to ask, or even say a word to him.

Late in the evening, as customers began to leave, another man who had been sitting at the bar all night began to speak to her. He was drunk, she realised, when he asked her out. She smilingly refused, praying that he wouldn't be difficult, used to handling men like him. But he was difficult. He grabbed her arm as she passed him on her way to serve someone else.

'Come out with me tonight,' he said again, the words slurring, eyeing her with an undisguised lust that frightened her, even though she knew it was the alcohol talking.

'Please let go of my arm,' she said politely,

wondering whether she should call for Philippe. But before she had time to decide, Luke was there.

'I think it's time you were leaving,' he told the man pleasantly in perfect French. But there was something in his hard eyes, something beneath the calm tone of his voice, that had the drunk on his feet in seconds, as though he was a puppet and Luke the puppeteer.

'I didn't know she was with you,' the man muttered as he walked unsteadily away.

'Thank you,' Stephanie said quietly in Luke's direction. She didn't look at him, she watched the drunk leave.

'What the hell are you doing working here anyway?' The anger vibrating in his voice jerked her eyes to the blank depths of his.

'It's a job,' she replied defiantly. 'I like it.'

'Oh yes, I can see that.' There was a hard mockery in his face.

'What are you doing here?' Stephanie whispered, hurt by his cold fury. Luke didn't answer for a moment, his wide shoulders very tense.

'Drinking too much whisky, I guess,' he replied at last, a faint smile playing at the corners of his mouth. Stephanie saw that smile, her eyes drawn to it, and relaxed with him. She was glad to see him, so very, very glad.

'Another coincidence?' she persisted, staring at him.

'Does it matter?'

'I never know where I stand with you,' she complained with a sweet frown.

'I don't think you'd really like to know,' he told her with dry certainty.

'No ... no, you're probably right,' she conceded, trying to read the unspoken meaning in his eyes. 'How long are you staying?'

He smiled, his eyes suddenly cynical. 'As long as I need to.'

'What does that mean?'

'You know damn well what it means,' he said softly, and swallowing back his Scotch, he turned and walked out of the restaurant, leaving her staring after him open-mouthed.

'Made a date?' Françoise's curious voice cut into her thoughtful reverie.

'What?'

'The gorgeous man in the green shirt, you clever girl!'

'I already know him,' Stephanie explained quickly. 'He's a friend of my half-sister's.' She had to remember that.

'You didn't say!' Françoise reproached laughingly.

'Didn't I?' The restaurant was closing up and Stephanie busied herself with the empty glasses, not wanting to talk about Luke, not even to Françoise.

Later, as she lay in the darkness of her room, half listening to the noise from the street below, she smiled to herself and whispered his name. He was here in Cannes, and that made her happy. Too happy for it to last, she had no doubt, but happy enough for now to drift into a deep calm sleep.

Luke came to the restaurant every night after that. He did not push her in any way. He seemed to be holding back deliberately. Sometimes he would eat and other times he would sit at the bar drinking whisky.

They didn't talk much, and when they did, he was gentle and charming, never asking anything of her.

They were like strangers, polite acquaintances, except that whenever she looked into his eyes, she saw an unspoken question that she could not understand burning there.

She began to desperately look forward to his arrival every evening, her heart pounding when he stepped through the door, so big and powerful and graceful. She had no idea what he was doing, but she knew that she needed to see him.

Four days after his arrival in Cannes, he was sitting at the bar reading a newspaper, when Stephanie noticed a slender blonde woman approaching him. She had seen the woman before in the restaurant. Françoise knew her vaguely. She was a rich American, and her husband had a yacht anchored in the harbour.

Stephanie's hand froze on the glass she was wiping as she watched the woman smiling. She was breathtakingly beautiful and Stephanie felt an irrational stab of hatred for her.

Luke was smiling back at her, his green eyes lazy, amused. The woman sat down next to him, her slim body swaying towards him provocatively, her red-tipped fingers lightly touching his arm. Stephanie felt her teeth snapping together. They were waiting to be served and she knew that she had to do it.

Pursing her lips, she walked over to them. The beautiful American ordered a Martini, Luke a whisky, his eyes amused on Stephanie's tight mouth. She poured the drinks with a blind red fury beating in her brain and had to stop herself from slamming them down on the counter.

Luke smiled, murmuring his thanks, reading her fury so easily, and she glared her anger at him uncaringly before turning away, her fists clenched at her sides.

But she couldn't keep her eyes off them for long. She had to know what was happening. Finally she looked, discreetly. They were talking, the beautiful American laughing at something Luke said, her golden head bent too near his shoulder. She was bored and predatory, and Stephanie hated her.

She watched them all night, talking and laughing together. She watched Luke's hard-boned face, the faintly cynical charm in his eyes, the amusement twisting his firm mouth, and angry pain tore at her. He knew the woman was married, he knew what she was offering, and irrationally, Stephanie prayed he wouldn't take it.

Then suddenly the truth hit her so hard that for a moment she couldn't breathe. She was jealous, green with spiteful jealousy. The very thought of Luke taking that woman back to where he was staying—and Stephanie didn't even know where that was—and making love to her, brought a pain that was almost physical. The images rolled with cinematic starkness through her mind, refusing to be banished, until she felt like screaming.

Later, she couldn't remember how she managed to get through the remainder of the evening. Despite all her efforts not to, she found herself watching Luke and his blonde companion closely, until as the restaurant began to close, they both stood up, and to Stephanie's angry horror, left together.

She watched them go, tears filling her eyes. What did you expect? she asked herself furiously. Did you expect him to turn down what that woman was so blatantly offering?

She had to get out of this place, she needed some air.

Philippe stopped her as she made for the door. 'Made your mind up yet?' he asked, with a peculiarly sweet, persuasive smile.

Stephanie had to think for a second, before she realised what he was talking about.

'Yes,' she heard her own agreement with surprise. 'I'd like to go out to dinner.'

It was an act of pure defiance. She was trying to

prove to herself that what Luke did was no concern of hers. She was trying so damned hard—and getting nowhere.

Philippe was pleased. 'Tomorrow?' he pressed gently, his eyes bright, triumphant.

'Yes, tomorrow would be lovely.' She tried to inject some enthusiasm into her voice, but failed, already half regretting the stupid impulse that had let her agree. 'I'm just slipping out for some air.'

'Shall I come with you?' He was gallant, concerned.

'No, thanks.' She was touched by his concern. He was such a nice man and she didn't want to hurt him with her lack of enthusiasm.

'Be careful, then,' he warned, and touched her cheek with his fingers.

'Of course I will.' She didn't know what he was warning her about and she didn't care.

After the hectic pace of the evening's work, she just needed some peace and quiet. She needed to find out why the sight of Luke with another woman filled her with such jealous anger. She needed to find out why she needed to see him, why she thought of him constantly. She'd had her chance—she'd turned him down flat.

She walked into the bright noisy warmth of the street, totally unaware of her surroundings, her mind spinning in fast circles, and towards the Croisette beach. She stared out across the brightness of the bay of La Napoule. It was a clear night and the brightly lit town of Cannes stretched out before her in a wide arc. She stared at it with eyes that did not register a thing.

She was thinking about Luke, concentrating fiercely. And when the answer came, it was even more shocking than the discovery of her jealousy.

She was in love with him. She had been in love with him ever since that first moment she had seen him at the traffic lights at home. Not the brotherly love she felt for Dean, but a fierce, all-encompassing love, that would grow stronger and stronger as time passed. She would never stop loving him, and this revelation answered all her worries about the way she had been acting.

Subconsciously she had known that she could never marry Dean. It hadn't been deliberate, or expected, or planned. She hadn't even known what love was until she met Luke.

She remembered the way she had always responded with such abandon to the touch of Luke's mouth, the stroke of his hands. At the time it had shocked her, filled her with guilt, but now she knew she had been fighting a love stronger than herself. She had never had a chance. She stared across towards the inky invisible horizon. She didn't know what to do. Luke was here in Cannes; at this moment he was probably in another woman's arms. And there was Carina.

The hopelessness of it all depressed her, but she couldn't keep running for the rest of her life.

'You shouldn't be out alone at this time of night.' Luke's voice made her jump. She turned to find him just behind her and couldn't believe she wasn't dreaming.

'So I've been told,' she replied with a smile, her heart somersaulting as she looked at him.

'You never do take good advice.' He stared down at the vulnerable lines of her face. There was laughter in his eyes.

Stephanie looked away, wondering where the American woman was. 'Your friend . . .?' She couldn't keep the sarcasm or the curiosity out of her voice, and she bit her lip, anxious not to reveal her terrible jealousy.

'Gloria? What about her?' Luke queried calmly.

Stephanie almost smiled. She should have known the woman would have a name lik Gloria!

'Oh, nothing. I just thought——' She broke off, shrugging.

'You just thought I'd be making love to her by now,' Luke finished expressionlessly, reading her mind so easily.

Her flushed cheeks gave her away, even though she said, 'I don't care what you do—you certainly don't have to explain yourself to me.' But in truth she was dying to know what was going on.

Luke's long fingers caught her chin, tilting up her face, so that he could see her carefully veiled eyes. 'What did you think of her?' he asked, smiling slightly. He was playing some sort of crazy game with her. She could see the mockery in his shadowed green eyes and felt angry.

'She seemed. . . .'

'What, Stephanie?'

'Well, if you want the truth, she's married.'

'I know that.' His voice held a soft amusement.

'Oh, I see, it doesn't make any difference if a woman is married,' she snapped, furious because he was laughing at her.

She felt the cool pressure of his fingers against her soft skin with a fiery pleasure that angered her even more.

'She knew what she was doing,' Luke said sardonically.

'And that makes it right?' Stephanie was scathing even though she knew Luke was speaking the truth. The lovely Gloria had been making all the running.

'Jealous?' he queried laughingly.

'Never! But I do think you should be ashamed of yourself,' she retorted icily.

Luke laughed again, his eyes holding hers. 'Shall I tell you what happened?'

She wanted to say no, she wanted to throw any explanations back in his face, but somehow she couldn't. She remained angrily silent as he continued.

'I took her back to her husband's yacht. She asked me on board——'

'I don't want to know!' Stephanie cut in desperately, afraid that she could not hide the pain in her eyes from him.

'You're going to know anyway,' Luke replied impassively, and the tautness of his face silenced her immediately. 'Her invitation was obvious. I refused it, politely said goodnight and left.'

Stephanie stared up at him in astonishment. 'Why?' she asked baldly.

'I didn't want her,' he replied expressionlessly.

'I don't believe you. She's beautiful!'

Luke shrugged his powerful shoulders. 'I don't find her at all beautiful.'

'You paid her enough attention tonight!' Stephanie shot back, unwisely she knew as soon as the words were spoken.

He smiled. 'You were watching?'

'I work there, remember?' Her mouth was a fierce stubborn line.

Luke didn't answer, but his eyes were wise and amused, and her anger grew.

'And I still don't understand why you didn't want her. I can't imagine *you* not taking what was offered.' She was lying, of course, trying to get to him because he had hurt her. He had his choice of women, he would choose his lovers selectively.

'What are you after, Stephanie?' he asked sardonically.

'I don't know what you mean. . . .'

'I think you do, and if it's that important to you, I'll tell you.' His eyes met hers, blank and unreadable, and she felt a tiny shiver of apprehension prickling along her spine. She really didn't have any idea what he was talking about, but she knew that the mood had suddenly changed, and tension spun between them. The raw mercurial atmosphere frightened her.

'Luke——' she began tentatively, but he didn't allow her to finish.

'You've been in my blood for a long time now,' he said broodingly. 'Why the hell do you think I'm here? I want you, Stephanie, and however hard I try, I can't get you off my mind for a single damn second. You've always known that, but now I'm going to spell it out. Since I met you, there has been nobody else—I can't touch another woman without thinking of you, without wanting you instead of her. I wake every morning with your name on my lips, sick because I'm alone, because I can't turn my head and find you next to me. I dream of touching you, of possessing you, every night I lie alone, aching with longing for you. Goddammit, there is only you, Stephanie.' He laughed humourlessly. 'And you ask me why I didn't accept Gloria's invitation to sleep with her?'

Stephanie stared into his face, seeing the stark, naked violence there, and began to shake—her whole body rigid with shock. The truth of his words was burning in his hooded eyes, and an aching weakness flooded her lower limbs. She didn't know what to say to him, her mouth was dry, her throat aching with tension.

Luke searched her wide eyes for long moments before releasing her and moving away to stand staring out over the bay in tense silence. Stephanie swayed as he released her, gazing at the broad tense sweep of his back, at the proud set of his dark head, her heart thumping.

His harshly-spoken words were still ringing in her ears, the rest of the world, the rest of reality, spinning crazily around those words.

'And now you know.' He did not turn round, his quiet voice laced with mockery.

Stephanie licked her lips, afraid to move. She wanted him so badly, even though she knew that he didn't love her. He would never be hers, but she had the chance of becoming his lover. He wanted her now, and could she really ask for anything more than that? She would want him for ever. For her, there would never be anybody else.

She made her decision on the spur of the moment, knowing it to be right, swayed by her deep love for him.

Slowly she walked over to him, on legs that shook violently.

'Can I ask you something?' she whispered, staring at the hard uncompromising lines of his profile.

'What is it?' he asked expressionlessly.

'Are you ... are you going to marry Carina?' Her voice was shaking.

'No.' It was immediate, definite, a little surprised, and he turned to her, his glittering eyes questioning. It was the truth.

'I want you, Luke,' she said quickly and clearly, before he could voice the question. She heard the hiss of his indrawn breath, saw the flaring of light in his eyes.

'Stephanie——' His voice was very deep, husky.

'Take me back with you,' she said softly. 'Make love to me tonight—please, Luke!'

There was a moment of electric silence, while his darkening eyes searched hers, asking her silently if she was sure. She was.

'I've waited so long to hear you say that,' he said with rough tenderness.

His strong hands reached for her with an urgency he

could no longer conceal, the warm hunger of his mouth, as it touched hers, sweeping away any last lingering doubts from her mind, making her sure, so very sure that she was doing the right thing, the only thing. It was a night for taking what you needed—and they needed each other.

CHAPTER TEN

LUKE was staying on a yacht in the harbour. It belonged to a friend. It was enormous and very luxurious, a sleek navy blue, with every modern convenience imaginable. Stephanie looked round as Luke fixed drinks, marvelling at the sheer size of it, the elegance.

They were in a long wide cabin, rows of traditionally-round portholes on both sides. All the furniture was fixed, stabilised against bad weather, the dark mahogany table edged with a rim of brass to stop things sliding off.

Everywhere she looked she saw deeply-polished wood, shining brass, the chairs upholstered in rich midnight blue velvet. She couldn't believe the size, the careless luxury of everything. It was like a five-star hotel.

'It's beautiful!' she said breathlessly, turning to him with a nervous smile.

'Yes.' He was staring at her with narrowed eyes, taking in the tension of her slender body, her wide fear-tipped eyes. 'Sit down,' he said gently, passing her a glass.

Stephanie perched nervously on the soft velvet, and instead of sitting next to her, he sat down opposite. She sipped her drink too quickly, glancing hungrily at the wide line of his shoulders, the contracting muscles in his brown throat as he swallowed his whisky.

'Where is your friend?' she asked, not looking at him.

'He's on business in Paris.' Luke reached out and touched her silken hair. 'Stephanie, relax.'

She nodded mutely and for a few minutes the silence built up again. It was so quiet that she could feel her heart pounding in her ears.

Luke watched her, his eyes unreadable, then suddenly he got to his feet.

'I'm going to take you back to the restaurant,' he said expressionlessly.

Stephanie looked up at him in startled surprise. Was he rejecting her?

'Why?'

He sighed heavily. 'It's not going to work, is it?' There was a faint smile touching the corners of his mouth.

'You don't want me?' she queried painfully.

Luke drew her to her feet, his hands curving gently over her shoulders. 'I think I want you too much,' he said with wry gentleness. 'You're so nervous, so beautiful—I shouldn't have brought you here. I suppose I was trying to rush things, afraid that you would change your mind. Come on.'

She let him take her hand, and as they walked out on to the deck, her throat became blocked with aching tears, and a disappointment so strong she wanted to die. She couldn't let it end like this.

She pulled her hand out of his and walked to the rail, staring across the reflection-filled water to the other yachts and boats, some noisy and brightly-lit. The sky was dark, the stars twinkling, and a faint scented breeze lifted her hair and cooled her hot cheeks.

She wanted to stay with him. She needed to stay with him. She turned to find him watching her, and she looked at him, her mouth dry. He was so big, so powerful, and she loved him so deeply. Without conscious thought, she moved towards him, lifting her hands to his shoulders and putting her mouth to his. 'Don't make me go back,' she murmured urgently, against the firm warmth of his lips. 'Take me to bed.'

For a second Luke did not respond and she felt in him a slight hesitation. Then suddenly he began to kiss her hungrily and she knew, as her lips parted beneath the pressure of his, that he could not control or deny his desire for her.

She held nothing back in her response to the bruising passion of his kiss. There was nothing to hide any more except her love for him, and she matched his need with her own. His arms tightened, moulding her to the aroused hardness of his body, his mouth moving deeply on hers, until at last he raised his head, his breath quick and uneven.

Stephanie bent her own head to his shoulder, trembling, a heated desire shivering through her body. But he gently pulled back her head, forcing her to meet the glittering depths of his eyes. He needed to be sure.

'Stephanie.' He said her name deeply, and she looked at him then, her face flushed with wild colour, her eyes dark with passion and with love. Luke read her answer and she heard him groan deep in his throat, before his mouth found hers again. She clung to him as the only stable thing in a crazily spinning universe. She was drowning in the deep hungry sweetness of his kiss, her blood boiling in her veins, all her senses filled with him.

When he finally lifted his mouth from hers again, it was only to lift her into his arms and carry her effortlessly inside, to a huge soft bed, bathed in warm light from a lamp overhead. He laid her down and arched over her, his mouth the touch of flame at her throat, at her bare shoulders as he deftly unbuttoned her blouse and pushed it away, his tongue tracing the fragile line of her collarbone.

He undressed her completely, his mouth moving against the bare skin he uncovered. Stephanie gasped with pleasure as he kissed her breasts, her stomach, then his lips moved lower, becoming more intimate, touching and caressing every inch of her body before he raised his head again.

'You're so lovely,' he murmured huskily, his dark eyes sliding the length of her naked body. 'Your skin is like satin—Oh God, how I've wanted you!'

He kissed her briefly, then she watched him as he undressed, the soft light gleaming on the tanned power of his body. He was magnificent, tall and lean and undoubtedly male. Unashamedly, she let her eyes wander over him. Smooth muscular shoulders, a powerful chest matted with fine dark hair, a hard flat stomach, lean hips and long hair-roughened legs. She stared at him, her body writhing, her heart pounding, his male beauty robbing her of breath. And when he came down beside her, taking her in his arms once more, she moaned, arching herself against his nakedness, revelling in the hard strength of his body, touching him, kissing him, as he had kissed her, her fingers sliding on his smooth skin, tangling in the hair that arrowed past his stomach, lower and lower until he stopped her with his own hands.

'No,' he groaned against her parted lips, 'I can't wait any longer.'

He pulled her against him, caressing her, arousing her with expert patience, until she was mindless with ecstasy, ready to give him anything, everything he demanded.

'Luke——' she moaned, reaching for him when her need became an agony too much to bear, and they were both beyond the point of no return. He moved over her then, his clenched body parting her thighs, and she heard him murmuring deep endearments into her throat, as he finally possessed her.

Her body arched against the thrusting strength of

his, and when the climax came, she was barely aware of her sharp gasping cries of satisfaction mingling with his, she knew only the hot aching pleasure that exploded into a mindless ecstasy.

As her breathing slowed and she came back to her senses, she stared drowsily down at his dark head bent to her breasts, sweetly aware of the weight of his body across hers, the hammering of his heart striking down against her skin. She touched his hair with gentle fingers, stroking through the vital thickness of it. She felt as though she was floating, her body drugged with pleasure, weightless. Luke moved, still breathing heavily, lingeringly kissing her body before he rolled on to his back and reached for her, taking her into his powerful arms, so that her head was against his chest.

Stephanie slid her arm around his waist. His skin was damp with sweat, the scent of his body clean, male and erotic.

'Ah, Stephanie,' he said unsteadily, murmuring the words against her tousled hair. 'Nobody else could make me feel like this. You're so beautiful.'

She smiled, deeply pleased, lifting her head slightly to look into the glazed darkness of his eyes. 'So are you,' she said softly.

Luke returned the smile, his mouth gentle as it brushed hers. She felt tired, sensually lethargic, deeply satisfied. She couldn't keep her eyes open, and with a faint sigh, she turned her face into his bare shoulder and fell asleep.

She woke at dawn, refreshed and languorously happy, and opened her eyes to see Luke next to her, still sleeping, his arm still tightly around her.

Without moving, she looked into his face with wonder, seeing an unexpected defencelessness in its hard lines, seeing the dark stubble along his jaw, the dark lashes curved against his cheek. A deep emotion twisted inside her. God, how she loved him! Last night had been so beautiful, so fulfilling. She had guessed that he was an expert lover, but nothing had prepared her for the shattering pleasure of his lovemaking. He was her first lover—there could have been nobody else, there would never be anybody else.

A grey melancholy began to creep over her as she lay staring at him. He didn't love her, she was sure of that. Luke used words like need and want, but he never mentioned love. She had thought it would be enough, and it wasn't.

She had been in his blood, he had said. Stephanie closed her eyes miserably. She had to get away. He had the power to destroy her if she stayed. She loved him so much she would probably end up doing something totally humiliating like begging him to let her stay.

Everything seemed to close in on her as her thoughts ran on, elation fading away. She looked at her life, at the future, and saw nothing but despair. A life without Luke didn't promise any happiness, and despite the fact that his arm was coiled around her, she felt achingly lonely. The thought of getting up and going back to the restaurant, facing all the questions, didn't make her feel any better either.

She sniffed, realising that she was crying. She looked at Luke again. He was still sleeping peacefully. As carefully as she could, she tried to move his arm from her body, sliding from beneath it and crawling on to the floor. She looked back at the bed, holding her breath. He had not moved, and her glance lingered hungrily on his bare tanned shoulders.

She had barely been aware of her surroundings the night before, but now she realised that they were in a large cabin, the walls lined with wardrobes and shelves. Off the cabin was a fully-fitted bathroom with a built-in shower. Again there was wood and brass, an air of pure luxury, of no expense spared. Any other time Stephanie might have been curious to know what secrets were hidden behind the numerous doors off the narrow passageway outside. As it was, she didn't care.

She looked around for something to cover her nakedness and found a black silk dressing gown hanging behind the door. The tears were pouring down her face now, blinding her. The silk was cool against her heated flesh, the dressing gown miles too big for her. She didn't know what to do. Walking over to the portholes, she saw that the sun was rising, the sky tinged with pink. Should she dress and leave without a word? She felt so unsure of herself and she couldn't stop crying.

'Stephanie, what's the matter?' She heard the deep concern in Luke's voice and looked round.

He was wide awake, sitting up crosslegged, watching her. She shrugged, unable to speak, and turned her head away. She should have gone when she had the chance, she thought dully. She didn't think she could bear any post-mortems of last night.

'Stephanie——' He was behind her, turning her to face him, his eyes skimming her tear-stained face.

'Leave me alone,' she whispered, as his touch shivered through her.

'Why are you crying?' he asked gently.

'I'm going back to the restaurant,' she said, sniffing loudly and ignoring his question.

'No, you're not,' he told her harshly, then as he looked at her, at her tousled hair, her slender body lost in the black silk, at her small bare feet, his eyes softened. 'What is it? Tell me,' he demanded quietly.

Stephanie wanted to go into his arms, the urge overwhelming her. She looked at the power of his body and her tears fell uncontrollably. What had she done? She would be trapped for ever by her unrequited love for him. One desperate impulse had trapped her for life. And suddenly all her misery and loneliness and insecurity froze into anger; anger at herself for being such a fool, anger at Luke because he seemed so untouchd by what had happened. She looked into his eyes, her face icy with defensive hostility. She wanted him to go away.

'Stop questioning me,' she said coldly, and shrugged away from him, walking across the cabin. I thought I loved Dean, she was thinking, as the wild irrational thoughts took hold of her, feeding on her insecurity. I was mistaken about him, I could be mistaken about Luke.

He watched her with narrowed eyes, his face tightening at her hostility. They stared at each other in heavy silence, the air between them filling with tension, with savage electricity. Stephanie's breath was constricted as she looked at him, her eyes wide.

'What the hell is the matter with you?' Luke demanded harshly. 'Last night——'

'I don't want to talk about last night,' she cut in desperately.

'Why not? It was beautiful—you were beautiful.' That dark gentleness was in his eyes again, fading into blankness when she retorted wildly.

'I wish it had never happened! I hate you! I wish I'd never broken off with Dean!'

It was a lie, a blatant lie, but for some reason she wanted to hurt him. She felt lost and confused and unsure of everything in her life.

Luke swore violently. 'You never wanted him—you know what sort of a man he is.'

'I don't care!' She glared at him furiously.

'So you regret the fact that we became lovers last night?' The violent savagery of his words shocked her.

'Yes, yes, *yes*. How many times do I have to tell you?' she shouted hysterically.

'Don't tell me, show me,' he muttered through clenched teeth, and strode over to her, tangling one hand in her golden hair and pulling back her head.

Stephanie looked defiantly into his glittering eyes, recognising the violence he was controlling with difficulty. She didn't fight him. She was going to show him that she didn't care. She had to make him let her go. But as his mouth parted hers, she felt that weakness running through her again, that aching need, despite the brutality of his kiss. She couldn't remain passive in his arms for more than a moment, and with a soft moan of surrender, she began kissing him back with a hunger that overrode his anger and fused them together with a fierce aching passion. Of their own volition, her hands came up around his neck, stroking greedily through his thick dark hair, stroking the tense nape of his neck.

She felt the abrupt hardening of his body, and gasped as his hands slid beneath the folds of black silk that covered her. He touched her bare skin with sure, gentle, arousing fingers. He caressed her slowly and hungrily, his palms closing over her naked breasts. He was shaking as he touched her, and when he reluctantly raised his head, iron self-control stiffening his body, she reached up and touched the firm beautiful line of his mouth, and whispered softly, 'Oh, Luke, I'm sorry.'

He took a deep breath. 'I can't let you walk away from me,' he said unevenly.

'You've got to let me go,' she replied quietly.

'Why?' Luke stared down at her, and she lowered her head.

'I don't want an affair with you.' Her voice trembled.

'It's a little late for that, isn't it?'

She flushed hotly. 'Last night was a ... was a mistake. I should never have let it happen.' She saw his mouth tightening ominously and said quickly, 'You know what I mean. I'm not the sort of person who has brief affairs——'

'I know that,' Luke cut in gently, and her legs trembled at the expression in his eyes.

'Yes,' she said quickly, very embarrassed, not wanting him to say anything else about her obvious inexperience. 'I'm sorry, Luke, but I think it would be best if I left now.'

'No.' He was cool and implacable, his arms folded across his broad chest. Stephanie swallowed nervously.

'How are you going to stop me? Are you going to keep me a prisoner here?' she demanded with husky defiance.

Impatience flared in Luke's eyes and he swore softly beneath his breath. 'If I have to.'

'Why won't you let me go!' she cried, almost afraid of him. 'There's nothing more to say.'

'I think there is,' he countered flatly. 'Last night was good, it was fantastic, good for both of us, Stephanie. We both knew it had to happen—we've known since the moment we first met, and I still want you. There's no way I'm going to let you walk out of here carrying all that guilt I can see in your eyes.'

'I *won't* have an affair with you,' she repeated, fighting hard. 'It may mean nothing to you, but I ... I. ...' She couldn't finish her voice cracking emotionally.

Luke moved towards her, but she held out her hand to ward him off. 'I don't know what to do in this sort of situation—it's never happened to me before. I didn't even know what I should do when I woke up

this morning. I didn't know whether I should leave
without a word, or wake you up or make coffee, or
what!' Her voice was getting higher and higher as she
became more upset. She didn't think she could bear it
if he touched her now.

Luke watched her intently for a moment, knowing
that she needed a few moments alone to get herself
together, then he said, 'I'll make us some coffee and
then we'll talk, okay?'

Stephanie nodded mutely, her throat blocked with
tears, thankful for his tact. As soon as he was gone, she
slipped out of the black silk dressing gown and quickly
pulled on her clothes, breathing deeply to calm
herself, and by the time Luke returned with a tray of
coffee she was outwardly collected and ready to face
him.

He smiled at her as he set down the tray, but his
powerful body was tense as he shrugged into his shirt.
The terrible tension was gone, Stephanie realised with
relief, as she gratefully sipped the hot, strong coffee. It
was all thanks to Luke's control of the situation. She
felt she ought to say something, but she didn't know
what, and as the silence lengthened, she felt his
brooding probing eyes on her face.

Finally, he said, 'I'm sorry—I've been acting like a
bloody fool. I didn't mean to upset you.'

She lifted her head. 'Me too,' she admitted wryly.
'But I meant what I said—I don't want an affair with
you. I don't know what I want. I've been so confused
since I broke off my engagement.'

She realised she shouldn't have mentioned it as soon
as she saw his eyes flaring with anger. He was
probably as unused to this situation as she was, she
thought, and had to hide a smile. The women who
ended up in Luke's bed were probably ready to settle
for anything he would give them.

'And last night?' he probed coolly. 'What was that? Pity? Pretence?'

'No,' she said earnestly. 'No.'

'Marry me, then.'

She heard the cool almost indifferent words with a pounding shock. She stared at him in astonishment, but his eyes gave nothing away.

'What did you say?'

'Marry me—it's a perfectly straightforward proposal.' There was a hard, almost wary edge to his voice.

'You don't want to marry me, any more than I want to marry you,' she said tremblingly, unaware of how insulting she was being.

His eyes became blank, as her words hit home. 'I want you, Stephanie, and I'm prepared to go to any lengths to get you,' he told her in a roughly violent voice. 'You wanted me last night, you still want me—and I can prove that to you.'

He was mad, she thought wildly, not listening to him. Why, oh, why hadn't she left when she had the chance? What was holding her here on this luxurious yacht, with this tall, handsome, green-eyed man who had become her lover only hours before?

She already knew the answer. His sheer physical presence held her. She loved him deeply, and if his proposal had meant anything more than an expression of desire, she would have accepted it immediately. As it was, she felt it was almost an insult, that he was trying to placate her into bed again. And she wasn't going to stand for that.

'You don't have to prove anything,' she told him angrily. 'I——'

Before she could say another word, the cabin door swung open and a slender, ravishingly beautiful woman appeared on the threshold. She did not appear to notice the awful tension in he room, she was looking at Luke, her admiration obvious.

'Sorry to barge in, darlings,' she said in a high breathless voice, obviously put on, Stephanie thought unreasonably.

'What is it?' Luke's voice was hard with impatience, but far from putting the woman off, it seemed to attract her more. She stepped into the room, ignoring Stephanie completely.

'You're Luke Baroda!' she said in husky surprise.

Luke nodded unsmilingly. 'We're busy. What do you want?'

She wasn't getting the message at all, Stephanie thought wryly, or maybe she was just ignoring it. But she was beautiful, with long auburn hair cascading to her waist and tiny yellow shorts that didn't hide an inch of her long tanned legs. How could Luke be unaffected by her? Stephanie wondered as she watched them both. It probably happened all the time. He would be well used to women flinging themselves at him.

'I'm looking for Bryan,' the woman said softly, her low voice grating on Stephanie's nerves.

'He's in Paris,' Luke revealed shortly. 'He won't be back for at least a fortnight.'

The woman's face registered no disappointment and she made no move to go.

Pursing her lips, Stephanie got to her feet. 'I'm leaving,' she said quietly to no one in particular. She wouldn't stay to watch this beautiful woman drooling all over Luke!

'Sit down,' Luke commanded, his eyes as hard as ice. She obeyed without thinking, sinking back weakly on to the soft bed.

He turned to the auburn-haired woman. 'You'll have to excuse us,' he said harshly.

'Of course.' Something in his voice had the woman

walking from the cabin in seconds, pausing only to flash him a devastating smile as she left. She intended to come back, Stephanie was sure of that, and jealousy filled her.

'Thank God!' Luke muttered irritably, as the door closed and they were alone again.

'She was beautiful,' Stephanie said coolly.

His dark brows rose sceptically.

'I suppose that happens all the time,' she continued, not looking at him.

'What?'

'Beautiful women falling at your feet,' she replied critically.

He laughed, and the open amusement in his eyes turned her heart over. 'You're not falling at my feet!'

'I'm not beautiful,' she snapped, angry now.

'You know that's not true,' he told her softly. 'And I meant what I said last night—there's been nobody since I met you.'

'And before?' Stephanie didn't know why she was asking. His answer would only hurt her.

'I'm thirty-six years old—I haven't lived a life of celibacy,' he told her with a shrug of his powerful shoulders.

'Why have you never married?' she asked. 'Have you never been in love?'

'I'd never found a woman I wanted to spend the rest of my life with.'

The tense he used and the darkness of his eyes had her rigid with shock. 'No——' she whispered unbelievingly, and unable to bear the strain on her stretched nerves, or the clattering silence, got to her feet, walking away.

'I wasn't joking when I asked you to marry me,' Luke said tautly.

Stephanie shivered, as white as a sheet. 'Why should you want to marry me?' she whispered.

'Because you don't want an affair and because, dammit, I don't either.' He was moving, his voice getting nearer. 'I want everything, Stephanie—I love you.'

She felt the coolness of his breath on the nape of her neck as he murmured his words of love.

'Why didn't you tell me before?' she asked shakingly.

'I told you last night with my body,' he replied deeply. 'I thought the words might frighten you away.'

He slid her arms around her waist, pulling her back against the hard warmth of his body. Stephanie relaxed against him, a brilliant happiness running through her.

Luke drew an unsteady breath and turned her in his arms. . . .

'Luke——' She whispered his name, staring into his lean face, seeing his love smouldering in the darkness of his eyes.

'I love you,' he repeated softly, his mouth hungrily sensual. 'And whether you like it or not, Stephanie, you're going to marry me.'

She smiled, radiantly happy, hardly able to believe it. 'How long have you loved me?' she demanded artlessly, sliding her arms around his waist, delighting in his immediate response.

'I guess ever since your father showed me your photograph,' he admitted with a rueful smile. 'You never had a chance after that. There was something about your eyes—a beauty that caught my attention. I wanted to meet you, I wanted to know you, and knowing what I did know about Sangster and the money he'd conned out of your father, I was bloody furious when I found out you were engaged to him.'

'You thought I was involved,' she remembered painfully.

Luke shook his head. 'I couldn't really believe it. I thought Sangster was using you, so I decided to fly out there.' He smiled wryly. 'God knows, you knocked me sideways the moment I saw you.'

'At the traffic lights?'

'Mm, at the traffic lights. I was obsessed with you from that moment on. I was desperate to get you away from Sangster before it was too late.' His voice was rough with a possessive desire that shuddered through her body.

'And if we had been lovers, if I had been involved?' Stephanie asked curiously, Luke shrugged.

'I don't know, I loved you and nothing could have changed that.'

'You told me it was all a coincidence,' she accused laughingly, secure now in a love that was so deep, so fierce and all-encompassing that nothing would ever break it.

'A man's entitled to a little pride,' Luke told her drily. 'Especially when the woman he loves is fighting him every inch of the way. Dear God, Stephanie, if you only knew what torment you put me through the day we had that picnic!'

'I thought you were rejecting me,' she said softly.

Luke closed his eyes. 'It was the hardest thing I'd ever done in my life, leaving you like that, but I knew you would hate me if we made love—you seemed to hate me.'

'I was afraid of you,' she admitted, her eyes meeting his.

'Why?' Surprised, he touched her cheek, his long fingers gently stroking her skin, a lover's caress.

'You turned my safe happy world upside down. Every time you looked at me . . . every time I looked at you, I wanted you,' she admitted, soft becoming colour flushing her cheeks.

Luke laughed, low and exultantly, his arms tightening until she could hardly breathe.

Stephanie thought for a moment, then said, 'So my visit to England . . .?'

'The solicitors helped me. It was the only way I could think of to get you away, I was even willing to tolerate Sangster in my house if it meant that you were there,' he admitted with an unrepentant smile.

'You didn't plan what happened between him and Carina?'

Luke shook his head. 'I wouldn't have hurt you in any way.' His eyes held hers.

'And what about Carina?' Stephanie probed, her mind spinning with all he had told her.

'What about her?'

'Well . . . well, she told me that . . . that the two of you were practically engaged,' Stephanie revealed, reluctantly.

Luke swore under his breath. 'There was never anything between us,' he told her truthfully. 'Oh, I took her out a few times, but it meant nothing. I was a friend of her father's—your father's, that's all. I guess she must have realised how I felt about you and tried to put a spanner in the works.'

'She's in love with you,' Stephanie said quietly.

'No—in love with my money, maybe, but not with me. She's in Scotland with Wayne at the moment. They say it's a big romance.'

Stephanie smiled, glad for Wayne. 'Really?' She wasn't just asking about Scotland.

'Really.' Luke touched his mouth to her forehead.

She looked into the glittering green depths of his eyes and believed him. He had never lied to her, she knew that now. Everything was so perfect, so beautiful, she could hardly believe it.

'Oh, Luke, I thought you'd not carried the business

of my father's embezzlement any further because of
Carina,' she told him jealously.

'It was for you,' he said simply. 'Everything was for
you.'

She smiled up at him and heard him catch his
breath. His mouth parted hers tenderly, his kiss
becoming deep and drugging and hungry as he felt her
response. Stephanie clung to him, drowning beneath
the pleasure of his mouth. Long minutes later, he
reluctantly raised his head and stared down at her with
smoky, unsmiling eyes.

'Tell me,' he muttered with harsh urgency. 'I want
to hear you say it.'

She touched his face. 'I love you, Luke,' she
whispered, the truth of the words shining in her eyes.
'I'll always love you.' She watched the muscles in his
brown throat contracting as he swallowed.

'And you'll marry me?'

'Yes, I'll marry you,' she agreed, her mouth very
gentle, very beautiful.

Luke sighed, heavily as though he had waited for
ever to hear her say those words. 'Ah, Stephanie,' he
murmured against her silken hair. 'You've been driving
me out of my mind the past couple of months! I can
hardly believe that you're finally mine.'

Stephanie laughed, the radiant happiness inside her
coursing through her veins like champagne, the world
full of rainbows.

'I was confused and unsure of myself,' she whispered
against his throat. 'I knew I loved you, but after finding
out what Dean was like, I had no confidence in my own
judgment. I thought I loved him once.'

Luke smiled, his jealousy gone. 'You were only a
child then,' he said gently. 'Your love for him was an
illusion. He was your father, your brother, but never
your lover or your husband.'

'I know that now,' she said, sliding her hand beneath his shirt and tangling her fingers in the hairs that roughened his chest.

Luke groaned, his eyes darkening passionately. 'I love you,' he said deeply. 'I'll love you until the day I die. And I need your love.'

Shaken by his intensity, Stephanie reached up and put her mouth to his. 'Take me to bed,' she murmured provocatively against the firm warmth of his lips, 'and I'll show you how much I love you.'

Luke lifted her into his arms and carried her to the bed, arching over her and parting her lips with a hunger that beat flame through her whole body.

In the seconds before she was completely lost, Stephanie suddenly remembered the restaurant.

'Oh no,' she whispered worriedly, 'I'll have to get in touch with Françoise—she'll be worried.'

'Later,' muttered Luke, pushing the blouse from her shoulders.

'And I'm supposed to be having dinner with Philippe tonight,' she told him breathlessly, gasping as his mouth touched her breasts.

'The hell you are!' Luke told her possessively, his tongue tracing erotic circles against her bare skin.

'The hell I am,' she agreed, on a soft moan. 'Luke——' Her fingers clenched against the unyielding muscles of his shoulders, desire roaring in her veins.

'I love you,' he told her again as his lips claimed hers, a powerful magic spell that made her shiver in his arms. It was all she would ever need to know, it was everything she wanted.

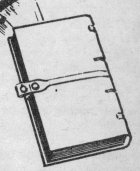